The Attempt

John Hopkins

The Attempt

New York / The Viking Press

First published in 1967 by The Viking Press, Inc.
625 Madison Avenue, New York, N.Y. 10022

Published simultaneously in Canada by
The Macmillan Company of Canada Limited

Library of Congress catalog card number: 67-13495
Printed in U.S.A. by Vail-Ballou Press, Inc.

A portion of this book first appeared in *Art and Literature,* number 11

For Joe McPhillips

The Attempt

i

We had been on this truck nearly the whole night, riding up on top where the trailer extends over the cab. There was a kind of low headboard and some boxes of vegetables to shield us from the wind; nevertheless it was so cold and uncomfortable that I had been unable to sleep at all. I lay on my back with my head resting on a lumpy burlap sack. I had a feeling beets were inside. Anne was lying beside me apparently asleep under her blanket.

From time to time I raised myself on my elbows in order to get a look at the sea. It was always there on the left, sometimes a mile or so away, sometimes only a few hundred yards. The line of breakers was visible in the moonlight. The coastal desert stretched away to the right, and beyond that rose bare round hills, now black, the beginnings of the Andes. I could make out the red glare of our tail lights and the dark road behind us. It's extraordinary how far one can see over the desert at night. Often I followed the lights of another passing truck until it seemed that ten or twelve miles separated us.

The pigs grunted occasionally. The truck was carrying, as far as I could judge, at least two hundred pigs. They had been crowded so tightly into two levels of the trailer that hoofs and snouts protruded through the wooden slats at all angles. When she saw them, Anne was somewhat reluctant to board this truck, but one of the drivers pointed to this place on top of the cab, and I persuaded her to get on. To me it didn't matter what the truck carried as long as we were riding up ahead of it.

Anne and I had spent the past two days and nights in some dry canyons and valleys about three hundred miles north of Lima looking for pre-Inca pots and artifacts in a burial ground she knew about. The place had already been partially excavated, but we searched around for anything that had been overlooked or forgotten and found intact some *huacos* and bits of coloured cloth among all the bones and skulls and wrappings. Anne is a kind of amateur archeologist, so the trip was an interesting one. Besides that I enjoy the desert landscape although I have a terrible time sleeping out there in those canyons. The ground is as hard as rock. I used to lie on my back the whole night with my hands behind my head, sniffing uneasily at the musty odour that comes out of those open graves.

I wasn't going to get any sleep this night either. The gusts of wind mixed in with diesel exhaust were too strong, and although I had a blanket and poncho, I was cold. One would think that desert air would be dry, but it's not always so in this Peruvian desert. I presume that this dampness is due to the proximity of the sea. Nevertheless, I must have dozed off towards dawn, for I recall glimpsing a lightness in the sky over the hills to the east.

What seemed to be a few seconds later came a terrible crashing noise and then the sound of Anne's voice shouting at me. She was dragging at my arm. I was in some sort of daze and believe my head must have collided with one of the boxes of vegetables which had partially protected us from the wind. Anyway, I managed to get to my feet among all the vegetables and climb down the side of the truck. But what a noise was coming from those pigs! I've never heard such a noise before. I've heard hundreds of pigs at feeding time but that sound was nothing to compare with what these two hundred were making.

By the time I reached the ground my head had cleared and I saw that we had run into the back of another truck. The sun had not yet appeared over the hills, but there was some light to see by. I took a quick look at the pigs. They were thrashing around so wildly inside their cage that I thought they would break down the wooden slats. I had to put my hands to my ears to keep out their screaming. Meanwhile Anne had jumped up on the running board of our truck and was peering into the cab window. She took one look and looked away and got down slowly, saying something I could not hear because of that pig noise. I stepped up and looked in. It was dark, but from what I could make out the other truck had been carrying long metal beams: I-bars and L-bars. These projected about fifteen feet from the back of that truck. When we went into it, the beams had come right in the windshield of our truck, passed through the cab just above the seat, and continued out the rear window and into the trailer behind, where they must have injured or killed some pigs. Thus that hideous screaming. I could see neither the driver nor his assistant through the mass of beams, but they were under them all right. Above the seat the beams were soaked with blood. The beams must have taken off their heads.

I stepped down. Anne was shouting in Spanish at two Indians who had appeared, apparently the drivers of the other truck. They looked scared and mumbled replies to her frantic questions. She turned to me.

"They were sleepy so they stopped their truck on the road to have a rest. On the road!"

She shouted at them some more. One just stood there, his wide face expressionless, the large mouth slightly gaping. He still looked sleepy to me. The other stepped up and looked into the cab; then his friend climbed up beside him and they peered in together. The pigs kept up their screaming, although not so loudly as before.

"They didn't even think to pull their truck off the road!"

"Our drivers must have been half asleep."

"They've killed themselves. It's so stupid!"

She was crying.

"Anne, are you all right?"

"I'm all right, Caffery. You didn't hurt yourself did you?"

"I think I bumped my head. Anne, you know we're lucky to be alive. So are those other two."

"Now all they want is to look at the dead men."

One of them reached inside, probably to touch the blood on the metal.

"They won't be able to see much through all those beams. Tell them to get back into their truck and pull it up, so we can find out what's happened inside."

She told them. The driver walked ahead to his truck and started the motor. When he began to move, our truck moved slightly with it; it seemed as if the beams would not become detached. The pigs commenced their shrill screaming once more. I looked back there again to see that one had been completely impaled by several beams and that many others were injured and bleeding. The blood was flowing off the truck and dripping down into large puddles on the road. I've never seen so much blood. At last the beams gave a lurch and began to pull free of the truck, dragging the impaled pig with them, its bowels slipping out through a tear in its stomach. It was finally forced off those skewers as they passed out through the hole they had made in the trailer. The dead pig dropped heavily on the wounded and the pitch of noise temporarily increased.

With a long grating noise the beams passed out through the cab and clear of our truck. I jumped up onto the running board and peered into the cab again. Our two drivers were in their seated positions, leaning slightly against one another with their shoulders just touching, like two lovers. Both had been decapitated. Blood and broken glass were everywhere. They were still bleeding. The blood welled up from where their heads had been and flowed down over their chests onto the seat and floor. Glistening in the early morning light, it appeared black. The assistant driver's left arm was still fibrillating against his companion's leg. I admit I had to turn away in order to avoid being sick. The two Indians came back and had another look.

Anne had sat down on the side of the road with her back to everything and was staring off in the direction of the sea. I went over to her

"Both drivers are dead. The beams tore their heads off."

Her body seemed to stiffen.

"Do you want to look?"

"No."

I noticed several pigs wandering around on the road and went back to the trailer to see where they were coming from. The metal bars had ripped open a large hole near the floor. Through this some of the pigs were leaving the truck, although it was partially blocked by the disemboweled pig and its slippery intestines. Three or four other pigs which had been injured now appeared to have died as well. They were all piled in there together, the live ones and the dead ones, with tails and ears pressing through the openings between the wooden bars. The noise had ceased, and they seemed strangely silent and unmoving. I must say these were some of the cleanest, fattest pigs I have ever seen. They must have been raised on cement, for there wasn't any dirt on them at all. Although they were all destined for the slaughterhouse in Lima, I was glad to see such a healthy lot of pigs. Each one of them must have been five or six feet long.

The sun had risen above the hills by now. The Indians squatted in the shade of their truck; Anne had not moved. I looked up and down the road, which was visible for about two miles in either direction, and saw nothing. The sea appeared to be about a mile away. The rest was just sand and rock and gravel. When the Indians talked softly to each other I felt grateful for the sound of their voices. For nothing better to do I climbed up on the truck and brought our gear down. This truck wasn't going any farther, that was for sure. From up there I saw about a dozen pigs out on the road. The day was already beginning to be hot, although it was still early in the morning.

I put the bags down beside Anne. "Are you sure you're all right?"

"Yes."

"You better not sit out here too long; it's going to get hot."

"Where shall I sit then?"

"In the shadow of the truck."

"Where? In the cab with the two dead drivers, or there with the two live ones?"

"Why don't you just sit next to the truck? You don't have to look at them."

"It doesn't make any difference to them whether you are dead or alive."

"Move back five feet and you'll be in the shade."

She picked up some pebbles and threw them down the embankment. "Did you hear them talking? They are afraid they'll lose their jobs if they arrive late in Lima."

"Perhaps they're right. Anne, what are you going to do?"

"I want to stay here."

I sat next to her for a moment before getting to my feet. I was feeling restless and wanted to keep busy. Flies were buzzing about the puddles of blood on the road and clotted on the dead animals' wounds. Streamers of half-dried blood which hung from the truck to the ground stretched almost imperceptibly when the air moved them. A great many pigs from the lower level had left the truck now, while the others above remained in their places, panting in the heat. A total of about ten pigs had been killed, it appeared, mostly from injuries, but there were some corpses without a mark on them. I suppose they had just died from fright or shock. As I took a closer look I spied the head of one of the drivers resting among the pig corpses. Rather than leave it there with the dead pigs I reached through the broken end of the trailer and grabbed it by the straight black hair and deposited it on the lap of the driver. In doing so I noticed the other head on the floor of the cab among the broken glass. I leaned through the open window and snatched up that one, also by the same rather oily hair, and gave it to the assistant driver. There was no telling which head belonged to which corpse. I assume I got it right.

About the same time I heard the sound of a truck approaching. It pulled up behind us and the drivers leapt out to run up and have their look. I went over to Anne again.

"Anne, do police patrol this road or not?"

"I don't know."

"I'm not going to wait around indefinitely. How can we get this accident reported?"

At last she got to her feet. "We'll have to report it ourselves."

"Then tell these drivers that have just arrived to go on and report this thing in the next town, so we won't have to stay here forever."

She told them, but they just nodded and went on speaking with the other drivers in their own language. It was at least an hour before they got back in their truck and drove off. In the meantime several other cars and trucks had stopped, so we had a curious little group examining the trucks and dead pigs and peering into the cab at the drivers. Some wondered at the heads placed so neatly on their laps, but I just kept my mouth shut.

I was crouching in the shade of our truck in spite of all the flies and the smell of animal and human blood. Anne had moved out of the sun and was sitting stiffly with her back against the front wheel. The day was beginning to stoke up. Silent mirages coated the land up and down the empty road. The blue water of the Pacific shimmered in the bright light about a mile away. I contemplated going for a swim, but a mile is a long way to walk in such heat—two miles it would be down and back and probably farther. On such days it is difficult to judge distances. Waves of heat rose from the land.

About ninety pigs were now free. In an attempt to escape the sun some were burrowing in the sand at the side of the road while others lay in the shade under both trucks. But it was clear they were having a hard time. They sprawled on top of one another and were breathing with difficulty. I was sorry to see them in such a state. From their appearance it seemed obvious that they had been carefully raised; their loss out here in the desert would be a waste of life and effort.

A mestizo truck driver who had stopped to inspect the accident came over and crouched down beside me in the shade. Together we looked out at the pigs moaning in the heat.

"Those pigs," he told me, "have no chance of surviving. Within twenty-four hours most of them will be dead."

"Why so soon? They're plenty big."

"In such heat they just dehydrate and die."

"Oh."

"I know those pigs. They come from a special farm in Trujillo."

"They're big and fat all right."

"Those are the best pigs in Peru."

"I've never seen bigger ones."

"Those pigs, they don't eat garbage. A special food is given them. I wouldn't mind eating it myself. Look how clean they are. They live in houses like people. Until now those pigs never knew what dirt was."

Towards noon the police arrived. They looked at our identity cards, asked a few questions, and took away the heads and bodies of the two dead drivers. No one seemed very concerned.

There didn't seem to be any point in remaining at the scene of the accident any longer, now that the police were handling the details. Therefore, we flagged down another southbound truck and asked if they would carry us to Lima. I don't believe that many of these Indian truck drivers have ever seen a European girl hitchhiking before, and whenever I travelled with Anne I never had any trouble obtaining rides.

This truck was carrying a heavy load of steel rods, the kind with which they reinforce concrete, and bags of cement. We sat up behind the cab to keep out of the wind and lit up some cigarettes. As the truck moved off, the wreck and wandering pigs began to shimmer and wobble in the heat and gradually disappeared among the mirages. I looked over at Anne. Her expression had not changed since the accident. She just sat there looking straight ahead. Anne had recently been widowed. While mountain climbing in the Andes her husband David tripped and fell a thousand feet to his death, dragging a companion down with him. When the others found him dangling on the end of his rope in a crevasse, they just cut him loose and buried his friend in the snow. I had a feeling she was thinking about him.

"I hate to see those pigs laid out like that," I said. "A truck driver told me they can't last long in that heat. They just dry up and die."

"Everything is wasted in this country."

"But most of the pigs are still alive. Perhaps someone will come along and rescue them."

"Wasted for nothing. I'm tired of it all."

"He said they were raised on a pig farm in Trujillo. Trucks delivering shipments of pigs must pass along this highway every day. Perhaps one returning empty from Lima will come along and pick them up."

"What a stupid way to die—to crash into a truck someone

has left parked in the middle of the highway while he takes a nap. Typical metallic death. It makes me sick to my stomach."

"This is supposed to be a very dangerous road."

"It's no wonder they don't react to death."

"Accidents like ours must occur all the time."

"Nothing could be more simple."

"What?"

"Death. It happens so easily."

I was beginning to think it was a mistake to have gotten on this truck. It was only travelling at about twenty miles per hour, and at this rate it would be past dark by the time we arrived in Lima. Even so, we were in no particular hurry, and the desert scenery is something to see, especially with the ocean glittering off to one side. It was plenty hot, however, and I wouldn't have minded a swim. Before long we came to a small town and the truck pulled up before a café. I was glad of this, for we hadn't eaten since the day before. This place was the usual roadhouse you find along this highway, with dusty bottles up on ledges before a rusty mirror, and cakes under plastic domes on the mosaic bar. Nevertheless, it felt cool and comfortable to be out of the sun and I ordered some *seviche* and a couple of beers. That tasted good. Then we had another course followed by dessert and pisco. It was a real banquet by the time we finished, but we needed it.

Back on the truck once more and I was feeling good after the meal. Anne seemed exhausted and attempted to sleep, but I sat up in the wind and enjoyed the ride. The driver swore we would be in Lima by sunset, which is a good time to arrive anywhere. I lit up another cigarette, as they burn down quickly on the windward side and don't last long, and watched the road tail away behind us. Everything seemed to move in the heat. Any dark object such as a mutilated truck tire writhed on the sand. Even the highway twisted and disconnected itself from the ground. The water shimmered so that I couldn't be sure whether it was the sea or one of those mirages the ground was all laked over with. From the mountainsides came the glint of sun off the rocks. The horizon fluttered and relaxed. The sun was hot, but the air felt clean and dry. As a matter of fact we were going along at just about the right speed.

Then we started passing these old-time billboards that someone had stuck out here in the desert years ago for no good reason. I saw the Lucky Strike ad with the old green and red package, and cola signs with girls in 1930s-style dresses and hair. They were all in good shape, too. The desert had preserved them just as it had those Inca mummies that we had been lately dismantling. It was a good ride, but I was beginning to wonder whether it required the sacrifice of two men and two hundred pigs to make me happy.

As the afternoon wore on we drew near the capital. More traffic appeared on the highway now, and our truck was constantly blowing its horn. The sun and blue sky and clear desert air dissolved under a low overcast. Although we would arrive at the usual hour of sunset, there would be no sunset in Lima. For six months of the year the sky over the city is obscured by heavy clouds and mist; yet it never rains.

Anne woke up shivering. We put on our jackets against the damp and disconsolately watched the endless slums and nondescript buildings, with smoke pouring out of factory stacks in the distance. Here on the outskirts of town comes the faint odour of fish meal from Callao. Besides, Lima has a peculiar smell of its own. I don't know what it is, but it's unmistakable if you've been here before. This must be the unhealthiest climate in the world.

We entered via Plaza Dos de Mayo where the trams rumble in and out to Callao, detoured along the River Rimac, and were let off on Abancay, near the bull ring. It was a Sunday evening after two days of fiesta, so the streets were full of people. Here I said goodbye to Anne, as she would be going in the opposite direction. She lived alone with her baby son in a tower located on an old Spanish estate right in the city. This was the first time she had ever been away from Jason and she was anxious to see him again.

"Caffery, be sure to soak those *huacos* in soap and water to get the desert salt out of them."

I told her I'd do it as soon as I returned to my room.

"Otherwise they eventually flake away in the damp and will be ruined."

"All right."

"The same for the cloth. It's full of salt."

Just then a boy said something in Spanish that I didn't quite understand. Anne yelled back and the boy disappeared. I could see that she was trying to forget her bitterness.

"Goodbye, Caffery."

I made my way through the masses of people along Abancay. There is an oriental flavour to this land. Perhaps I associate it with the passivity of these Indians. Here the explanation of their origin seems valid. Fat brown women sit before mounds of avocados, which they endlessly stack and polish with smooth old Indian hands. The men gather around charcoal braziers to watch *anticuchos* roasting on wooden spits. In the light of the flames their broad faces reflect a stillness amid the confusion. I paused to buy a newspaper and walked on through the smell of *anticuchos* and into the sounds of rambling tram cars with the squashed avocado peels slippery under my feet.

I was living in the Pensión Americana above the YMCA on Carabaya. You enter through great rotting Spanish wooden doors. On the far side of the stone court is a shoeshine stand where for two *soles* they will give you a twenty-minute shine —the best I ever got in Lima. Then up a long flight of saw-dusted marble stairs to the wood balcony, back through the laundry and pigeon coops to room número 6.

I took the pots out of the bag and put them along with the

cloth into the sink. One of them had a design of monkeys traced along the rim. Tiahuanaco, she had said. I ran the water over them and emptied in some powdered soap out of a box. Before unpacking the rest of my gear I put some music on. I've got a small record player with a fragile tone and a few records, mostly Peruvian music, some *tristes* and *huainos*. It gives me a good deal of pleasure. Sometimes a man by himself can occupy a very small space in a room. Anyway, I had a hard time setting the needle on the record without scratching it, my hands were shaking so much. That accident must have put me in a mild state of shock. After all, we might have been killed ourselves had the truck tipped over. Then I lay down on my bed with my hands behind my head to relax for a moment. I must have fallen asleep immediately, and when I awoke it was nearly eleven o'clock. The nap did me good though, for I felt refreshed and hungry.

I stepped out on the street again. A heavy mist was falling; a tram rumbled by. There were several good restaurants in the area, and now I had to choose which one. After some thought I decided on Rincon Toni's, a Swiss place. At least there they have red cabbage and good beer, which is what I wanted. Besides, it wasn't far away.

The proprietor, a heavy Swiss, gave me a sombre nod as I entered. I came to this restaurant nearly every night. Now with the exception of the waiters, himself, and myself it was totally deserted. I ordered the cabbage, the beer, and some pork, which for some reason I felt like eating. I had just finished and was about to ask for some coffee when in walked Paul Bonsal. He was a man who looked about my age, although in actual fact he was more than twenty years older. He had been living in Peru a long time and, according to his friend Antonio, knew the country as well as anybody and spoke the language better than most Peruvians. He was a great explorer of the Sierra and Selva, and always travelled alone. I had met him once or twice but

found him reticent and extremely difficult to talk to. I admit I
was a little nervous to see him here in this restaurant.

He came over to my table and sat down at my invitation. We
had a couple of beers together and talked about the jungle. Finally I said, "I'm going to have a cup of coffee. Do you want
one?"

"Let's not have coffee here; I know another place where they
serve the best coffee in Lima."

"Where?"

"I'll show you."

"Does it make that much difference?"

"Yes, it does."

I said to myself, Well now we're going to see something.

"All right then, let's go."

Bonsal had his old car outside. We drove across town to the
Plaza de Armas, where he parked next to the statue of Pizarro
across from the church. We got out and walked across the Plaza
in the heavy mist. It was late, past midnight, and few people
were in the streets. Bonsal was talking about the cathedral and
what a fine building it was although many criticized it for being
so low and squat, adding that the small edifice next to it was
even finer architecturally. We turned down Calle Unión. Bonsal
went on to say how much he loved this country and this city.
The mist was getting heavier, it seemed, and the footing became
slippery underneath. At La Merced church we turned left and
passed through some oak doors into a restaurant called Ray-
mondi's. The kitchen was off to the right, and I caught a
glimpse of the long wood stove. There were still several people
in the place, but more waiters than customers—old fellows who
stood around with their hands behind their backs. We ordered
the coffee. It was good, the best in Lima.

A man seated next to us was eating something that looked
good—ground corn and raisins and meat cooked in corn
shucks.

"Paul, what's that?"

"Pastel de choclo."

"I'm going to have one."

"All right, but not here. I know a spot on the other side of the river where they do them just as well, and it's a more interesting place besides. They have music."

"How do we get there?"

"On foot."

Now, I thought, there's going to be something big in store. "Let's go."

We were out in the mist again, thicker than ever, retraced our steps along Unión, across the Plaza de Armas, behind the Palace, and crossed the bridge over the Rimac to the other half of the city. Then we kept on straight for a while, turned left and into a little café-bodega. It had a dirt floor and barrels piled up higher than you can reach. Dirty cobwebs hung from the rafters and the bullfight posters on the walls were so old and dusty that you needed a flashlight to look them over. We sat down on a bench and ordered beers and those corn things. Bonsal was right, they were delicious. Behind the bar a record machine was playing this high-pitched mountain music. Bonsal fell right in with it and kept time with his hand on the edge of the table.

"I love this music," he said.

Bonsal began to talk. He had been in the navy during the war and had seen some action in the Pacific. A close friend of his had been killed. I sat back and listened to him and the music and drank my beer, which they served up in big brown sealed jugs. Suddenly he cut himself off and didn't say anything more. I signalled to the man behind the bar to bring us another jug of beer.

"No," interrupted Bonsal. "Come on, Caffery, I want to show you one more place."

"What place?"

"The Mercado Mayorista."

I'd heard about this before. It's a wholesale market in a rough part of town.

"It's a little late to go to the market."

"This is the only hour it's worth going out there."

"All right."

On the way back to the car he stopped in front of the railroad station. "Do you see that restaurant across the street—the one on the corner?"

"Yes."

"If you like liver and spinach it's the only place to eat."

"I'll remember it."

"The pisco is also the best."

"All right."

At this late hour I was surprised to see so much activity at this market. Trucks rolled in and out filled with all kinds of fruit and vegetables. Under powerful overhead arc lights they were being loaded and unloaded, with plenty of shouting and running around. Cafés lined the streets, and they were full up. We walked along looking at all these people going about their business until we came to a truck unloading crates of oranges. Bonsal went up to the man and bought a whole crate right on the spot.

"What are you going to do with all those oranges?"

"I like to have fresh orange juice in the morning. If you don't drink it within five minutes after it has been squeezed it loses all of its vitamin C."

I told him I'd never heard of that before.

He paid the man and hoisted the crate up onto his shoulder and carried it back to the car. Then he led me to this particular café he seemed to know about.

It was a noisy place filled with men, mostly truck drivers I guessed, and boys standing at the bar or sitting in booths along the wall, all drinking pisco. That same mountain music was coming from somewhere and the men at the bar were rubbing against each other or making signs to their friends across the room. There were two ugly girls at the bar, drunk, with their dresses coming apart. A few turned to look at us as we sat down in a booth but generally they just continued rubbing around in time to the music and this crazy signalling, as if they were all a bunch of deaf-mutes.

Bonsal ordered a bottle of pisco and a couple of glasses, and we began to drink it down. For a while we didn't speak, but watched the others in the café. Behind the bar was a cage full of animals. They looked like hedgehogs to me, but Paul said they were guinea pigs. Apparently they make good eating.

"Paul, what makes this city smell the way it does?"

"What smell?"

"Can't you smell it? It permeates everything."

"I know what you mean. I've been here so long I don't notice it any more. It must be the dust from the Sierra—the Indians bring it in with them mixed with their own sweat. All Andean towns smell the same."

"Sometimes I can't smell anything else."

"This is the worst time of the year for it."

"How much longer is this winter weather going to last?"

"Another month or so; then it clears up."

"All this perpetual grayness is getting me down."

"You'll get used to it."

"The fog depresses me. Sometimes when I get up in the morning I don't even want to go outside."

"It'll soon disappear. The summer sun burns it off."

"I've never been in such a silent city. The heavy mist seems to damp out all the noise. It's like a snowstorm."

"The *garúa*."

"What?"

"It's called the *garúa*."

"Oh."

The pisco was beginning to unloosen us by now. I told him about the pig episode.

He shook his head. "Be careful of that road. I don't know how many accidents I've seen on it. Look at these truckers in here. They get dead drunk on pisco, then climb into their trucks and drive off north and south on that highway."

We asked the waiter for another bottle. After you've been primed, it goes down like water.

"Do you feel like swimming?" asked Paul as we finished off the pisco.

"A swim? Now?" I was tired and looked at my watch. Three o'clock, and I had to be up at eight.

"Yes, now. In the Pacific."

"It must be cold."

"The water remains the same temperature year round."

"All right. Let's go."

I paid the waiter and staggered out after Bonsal. He drove so far out of town that I didn't know where I was. All I could see were the big hills in front of us. He talked the whole time, while I was having trouble keeping my eyes open. Finally we rounded one of the hills and went down onto a flat place and all of a sudden the whole Pacific was there before us. We stripped on the beach and plunged in. The water was cold and I woke up in a hurry. The big Pacific rollers tossed me around but the water smoothed out those bottles of pisco and beer. Back on the beach Bonsal said, "Let's run."

So we ran—about a half mile, it seemed, until I couldn't go any more. Bonsal kept on, then returned, and we ran the half mile back. We stood on the sand and talked for about ten minutes before putting on our clothes.

"How about coming back to my apartment for a drink?"

"Fine."

Bonsal lived in a flat that overlooked the whole city, which he had had ever since he came to Lima fifteen years ago. It was filled with all the things he had collected over the years: Indian ponchos, blankets, rugs, maps, clay pots and figures, and a live cactus hanging over the door.

"It brings good luck."

"How does it live?"

"On air."

On one wall he had a poster announcing the production of *Othello* by William H. Shakespeare.

"What's the H stand for?"

"The Spanish think everyone has to have a middle name."

He took off his shoes, and I noticed he had on yellow cotton socks with holes in both heels. This time he brought out a whole jug of pisco, which he drank like Kentucky mountaineers take their moonshine, finger through the handle, jug in the crook of the elbow. "From Ica. The best you can get."

I had my drink and we stepped out onto the terrace to look over the city. The clouds were so low that they seemed to rush by just a few feet over our heads. We watched for a few minutes in silence before I said I ought to leave. He replied that he would take me in his car. On the way back he talked about the car and, old as it was, how much he needed it and depended upon it to get around.

■ ■ ■

The next morning I had to get up early to go to work. I've got a job which I dislike, but it allows me to live in this country. For that I count myself lucky. At this time of year I don't like Lima very much either. This is the hour when I like it the least. In the dull light the city reveals its drabness. Often you see Indians straggling in from the Sierra in twos and threes, ponchoed, with shoes made out of old rubber tires. They stop to gaze blankly at window displays and continue on at a trot, coughing and spitting out their lungs onto the pavement. Overhead black vultures float and circle against a gray cloudy sky. Others peer down from perches atop billboards and buildings, looking at those bright red patches left behind on the sidewalk. It never rains here, but the heavy night misting leaves the streets slick with gray muck. This is the time when the smell is the worst.

I didn't see either Paul or Anne for some time and lapsed back into the old routine. The hours when I wasn't working I walked around the town or stayed in my room at the Americana, generally lying on my bed and listening to records. After a while, however, the sad fragile quality of that Indian music becomes monotonous, and I had to turn it off. Twice I went to the restaurant near the railroad station that Paul had pointed out. The liver and spinach and pisco were as good as he had said. I suppose I was hoping that he would make an appearance, but was disappointed. Afterwards I would go to a bar—anything to avoid returning to the pensión too early. I have difficulty sleeping, and living above the YMCA does not give me much peace. They play serious ping pong until midnight.

Returning from work one evening I got hung up in a tremendous crowd on the square opposite the University of San Marcos. Some sort of demonstration was taking place, but I couldn't make out exactly what it was. This plaza is where you can take a taxi, *colectivo,* or bus to all parts of the country. Now the people were climbing up and standing on the vehicles to get a better view. Some boys had even shinnied up the lamp posts. I was about to turn around and go back by another way when I spied Anne.

"Anne!" I cried. "What's going on here?"

"Caffery, what are you doing in this mob? The students are protesting against the government. I can't even get into the building for my class."

Anne taught an evening English class at San Marcos three times a week.

"What's the government done?"

"There's been trouble up in the Sierra," she shouted. "Some communists have issued false deeds to Cerro de Pasco's land."

"To whom?"

"To the Indians. You know that Cerro de Pasco owns vast tracts of sheep land up there."

"I didn't know that."

"The company says they need the sheep to feed and clothe their workers. But there are thousands of Indians who have no land at all."

"Oh."

"So these Indians broke down the fences and squatted on the land, thinking it was theirs. When they wouldn't move, the soldiers came and shot some of them. But I don't blame them."

"Who?"

"The Indians."

Until now the crowd had been noisy but calm. The students who were actually demonstrating were some way off. I could see some flags being waved around near the entrance to the University and heard the faint sound of chanting. That was only because I happen to be taller than the average Indian and could see over their heads. Anne, who is short, neither saw nor heard anything.

"It seems to be a mild protest," I told her.

All of a sudden there appeared from a side street a low gray machine, something like a homemade tank. I didn't know what it was but everybody else did, and began retreating in a hurry. Then from a nozzle on the turret a high-pressure stream of water was released on the crowd. A yell went up and everyone started to run. I looked back to see men and boys leap down from the roofs of cars and buses, slide down from the poles and trees they had climbed. Those who couldn't get down in time were knocked out of the branches like monkeys. However, most of them were not hurt, just wet and frightened. Behind the tank advanced a solemn phalanx of helmeted police, armed with billies. They routed those who had hidden behind trucks and statues. We had to run to keep from being trampled by the crowd until it was possible to take refuge in a doorway and look back. The plaza was now quite empty. The stream of water had been reduced to a flow which splashed aimlessly onto the pavement; around the tank the gray-uniformed police stood watching the crowd disperse. There had been no real violence, just a lot of people running away from a machine.

"They ought to have one of those tanks up in the Andes," I said. "Better than shooting them."

"They'd never be so humane as that. But let's get out of here."

We started walking. Out on the plaza the police closed ranks and marched off after the tank.

"Caffery, what are you doing now?"

"Nothing."

"Come home and I'll give you something to eat."

"What about your class?"

"I'll tell them I couldn't get in and went home. Anyhow, all the students have run away."

I was anxious to see where Anne lived. We went out past the new Ministry of Education building, which is so ugly I don't even like to look at it, turned up Abancay, and went off through such a labyrinth of side streets and back alleys that I wondered how I was going to get out. At last we came to a wood door in a high red wall which Anne pushed open. On the other side we were confronted with a forest of tall trees.

"What's this?"

"The estate. Come on."

We followed a path through the trees.

"How big is this place?"

"Enormous."

"Who owns it?"

"An old man."

She led me to a brick house all grown over with bushes and vines. Inside, an Indian family was seated around a table eating out of a large stew. They all greeted Anne and she stopped to talk to them before we continued upstairs.

"They wonder why I'm back so soon."

At the top of the stairs was a door, and we stepped outside once more, this time onto a flat tarpaper roof.

"Be careful. This roof has weak spots."

It groaned and gave so much under my first step that I thought I would plunge through right down to the bottom. Anne walked across, and I tried to see where she placed her feet. The trees grew so thickly about the house that I had to push their branches out of my way. At the far side was the tower with one small octagonal room inside.

"Is this it?"

"This is it, and this is Jason," she said, holding up the baby.

An Indian girl about ten years old was standing next to the bed. Anne said a word to her and she left. I looked around. This room contained all that Anne had: besides the bed there was a bureau, a chair, a table, and a crib. Along the wall were some shelves where she kept her collection of *huacos,* some books on history and archeology, and a few novels by South American authors. Ponchos and bunches of coloured candles hung on the walls.

"I like this tower. How long have you been living here?"

"A few months. Before that we had a flat near the Plaza de Armas, but it was too hot during the summer and Jason got terrible rashes."

"All these trees will keep you cool."

"Yes."

"Are there any animals in these woods?"

"Lots of birds, a few squirrels and rabbits. I think the old man brought them over from Spain years ago."

"Where's the big house?"

"On the other side. I'll show you later."

Anne fried some meat and bananas over a hot plate hidden among cans of powdered milk behind the door. Afterwards she brought out a bottle of pisco.

"Anne, do you plan to live here indefinitely?"

"I will unless the British government cuts off my widow's pension, which they've threatened to do if I don't return to the U.K."

"Can you live on that?"

"That and the three teaching jobs I have. It's a pittance. If I were alone it might suffice, but Jason is expensive. He's not even a year old, but already he costs more than I do to keep alive."

I got up and looked out the window. The shapes of the trees were moving in the darkness. "It's quiet here."

"I know."

"There's a dovecote outside my door at the pensión. Those birds flap around all night long."

"I can sleep anywhere. Noise doesn't bother me."

"You're lucky to be living in this tower."

"It's true, but I don't see how I can continue to live with Jason in this way."

"Why not?"

"We're too vulnerable. Before I was married it was all right: if I had no money I was broke. But I could live. When I was married it was all right. With Jason it's different. He's too much of a responsibility for me alone. I don't know what to do with him."

"As he grows up he'll be less trouble." I leaned over and poured out another glass of pisco.

"If I were a man I'd never get married."

"Anne, I think you're doing all right."

"I hope so. I'm glad you said that. But enough of a woman's problems. What about yourself? How much time are you going to spend in Lima?"

"Sometimes I think I'm ready to move out at any moment."

"Don't leave too soon, Caffery. You'll regret it. You haven't seen anything yet, just a Lima winter."

"I think I'll take a trip into the jungle before long. I want to see more of the country."

"Good. That's a good idea."

We made plans for another journey up the coast. She knew a pre-Inca site called the Valle de las Culebras, where we might make some interesting discoveries. We would go in a few weeks, when more fiestas would combine with a weekend to give us enough time to get out of the city for a few days.

I got lost on my way back and had to follow the tram tracks to Plaza San Martín. There I ran into Harry, an Indian boy who lives exclusively on that Plaza, as far as I can make out, sleeping alone on the grass or with anyone from the Hotel Bolivar who happens to pick him up. Harry has slightly Mongolian features, with high cheekbones pinching black cloudy eyes. He always manages to be well dressed and is always the same, penniless and talking bad English and inviting me to a cup of coffee. We sat down at a café under the arcades and discussed his passport, which was going to take him to Los Angeles. Harry had been expecting this passport for some time, and I wondered whether it would ever come. He was always talking about it.

When I finally reached the pensión, Bonsal was sitting on the other side of the court, having his shoes shined. I was glad to see him.

"What are you doing here, Paul?"

"Waiting for you. This is the fifth coat of polish he's put on my shoes."

"They do a good job here."

"I've come by to say that Antonio has invited you to dinner Sunday night."

"Fine."

"You know where he lives, don't you?"

"Yes."

He got up and paid the boy. "Then I'll see you Sunday."

"All right."

He crossed the court and went out through the heavy wood doors.

■ ■ ■

On Friday afternoon I called on Señora Davis, who is always glad to see me. Antonio had put me on to her a few months ago for Spanish lessons, but I never went regularly. She lives alone in a small flat near Plaza de Armas. Our conversation always starts out in Spanish. Gradually more and more English words creep in as I need them to express myself. She speaks English well and reluctantly gives way. In the end we are speaking mostly English with a few Spanish words thrown in when she is unable to express herself.

She brought me a *tapa* and a beer. I asked her how she was.

"Very bored. You are my only student and you never come any more."

I told her I was so exhausted after work that I just went back to the pensión and stayed here, which was not the truth.

"*Pobrecito*. Five years ago I used to give lessons at the American Embassy every afternoon and private lessons in the evenings. Now I have nobody but you. I don't care about the money; the money is nothing to me. All I want is something to take me out of this flat in the afternoons. It used to be such a pleasant walk to the American Embassy, especially during the summer. Now I don't walk any more, except to market."

She got up and brought me another beer. "From one Sunday to the next I talk only to the maid. Maria is a good girl, but her conversation is limited. I think I shall return to Spain. I have written my brother in Madrid."

Sra. Davis had left Spain during the Civil War. Her brother had sided with the Republicans, and Franco had jailed him for a few years.

"Soy la mujer más aburrida de Lima; I have nothing to do. I have a sister in Bilbao. Perhaps I'll go visit her."

I told her Bilbao is now a great industrial town. There are factories everywhere and the air is filled with smoke—worse than Lima in wintertime.

"My sister writes that the *barrio industrial* is removed from the city. There is no smoke where she lives."

She put on a record. Sra. Davis has a large record collection which she likes to talk about, but she never really listens while they are playing. They just give her something to talk about.

"In Alicante, the town of my birth, exist no factories of any kind. The weather is excellent, and I still have some cousins, though distant, who live there."

Before I left she gave me a *chorizo* which had been sent to her from Spain. She knows I like this Spanish sausage, which you can't buy here in Lima. Unfortunately, however, I left it in a bookshop on Calle Unión, where I stopped on the way down to the pensión.

I slept until noon on Sunday. To waste the rest of the day I took a *colectivo* out to the Archeological Museum, which Anne had been urging me to visit. That was closed, and I continued on to Herradura, one of the city's public beaches. No one was about, so I walked along the shore beneath some rocky cliffs. Great numbers of seagulls and pelicans were perched on the rocks. The sea mirrored the sky's grayness. At one point I had to step around the carcass of a horse that must have fallen over the cliff some time ago. Across the frame of its bones the hide was draped loosely like an old canvas. Probably those pigs were in a similar condition by now.

After an hour's walk I came to a deserted beach that swept in a wide arc between two jutting cliffs. The Pacific rollers were thundering against these cliffs with great force. As they receded the dark rocks streamed with white water and reflexive waves were set out to meet the oncoming swells. A foam line undulated peacefully one hundred yards from shore. With the sound of this dangerous surf in my ears I walked along the beach. A flock of brown pelicans rose in front of me and flew in a great circle over the waves to settle on the swell beyond the steaming cliffs. I passed by their place on the sand and saw their tracks and feathers and droppings. Beyond, a dead sea lion lay stranded.

I grew tired of pacing back and forth and climbed the far cliff, where I sat down and took a sandwich out of my pocket. I chewed on that for a while and looked out over the waves. Although the air was clear where I sat, a heavy fog veiled the sea a mile or more out. I sniffed at the air: these cliffs have an acid fish smell about them. Then the fog receded and to my surprise two ships were in plain sight. I guessed that they were headed for Callao.

When the mist began to envelop the cliffs I got to my feet and walked slowly back. I was glad I had somewhere to go. From Herradura a bus took me part way to Miraflores, where Antonio lives. I had two more hours to waste and strolled along the Pacific bluffs near his home. This is a peculiar section of Lima, presumably residential but with great empty spaces between the houses, dusty areas where boys shout and kick a ball around in the distance. A number of stray white dogs trot through the streets, constantly yapping at one another. Buzzards sweep the sky. I could hear my footsteps echoing.

The moment I was knocking on his door Antonio arrived from his school in Chaclacayo. We entered together. For the

next hour we listened to records and went down to the basement
to look at his impressive collection of electric trains. It was a
complicated arrangement but Antonio ran it all smoothly, with
a lot of noise and smoke. Shortly afterwards Paul arrived. We
had an *aperitivo* and sat down to dinner. Although Antonio is
fat his dinners are lean: this one consisted of one little piece of
roast chicken and dessert. I told Paul that I was considering
taking a trip into the jungle before long.

"You ought to. You should see the jungle. I'd like to go with
you."

"Yes, why don't you?"

"I can't. I've just come back from there. I can't travel all the
time."

"I wish you would. Where shall I go?"

"Take a river trip if you can, the Huallaga or the Ucayali."

"Are there boats?"

"Rafts, canoes, anything you can find. Otherwise you'll have
to fly and see nothing."

"What shall I take with me?"

"Something for insects. I've had to smoke seventy or eighty
cigarettes a day just to keep them off when I had no other protection."

"What else?"

"You'll need medicine for malaria, although that's no problem any more, and for dysentery."

"What about snakes?"

"You rarely see one."

"Good."

"The only time they really come out is about four o'clock in
the morning, to hunt along the river banks."

"I'll remember that."

"But above all travel as light as possible. Take some medicines, a few extra clothes, and put them into a rubber bag to
keep them dry."

"I don't understand why anyone wants to go into the Selva," said Antonio. "You find exactly what you expect—an unhealthy climate, too hot and too wet, diseases and insects and terrible animals. You're trapped under the trees. No civilization has ever been established in the jungle. The Sierra is far more interesting. There you have space over the land."

After dinner we had our coffee in the living room.

"The perfect life," said Antonio, "is two hours of reading, two hours listening to music, and the rest of the day spent with your friends."

When the time came to leave we walked out onto a small promontory and listened to the sound of the waves on the rocks below. To the north the lights of Callao were visible, and those of ships lying out at sea waiting to enter the harbour. I told Antonio what a strange part of town I thought he lived in.

"It is, and that's why I like it. Except on hot summer evenings when the moon is out. The dogs bark all night long, and I have to shut my windows."

Paul drove me home. In the car I remarked how thin the meal was, how fat Antonio. He explained that Antonio had an ulcer and ate practically nothing, and neither drank nor smoked. Formerly, however, he ate a great deal. I declared that I was still hungry. Paul said he would take me to a particular restaurant he knew about where they have the best fish in Peru, and turned down the road to Callao. I'd been to Callao a few times. There's always something going on at the port.

We walked into the restaurant and there were the fish, all spread out on a marble counter with seaweed and ice on them. You just step up and tell the man what fish you want and he gives it to the cook. I wasn't ready for a whole meal and chose a fish soup, which Paul said was a meal in itself. Judging from the number of crayfish, clams, and fish the man handed over to the cook I could see he was right. Paul ordered the same dish and we sat down in a booth with doors on it which you can close if you want to. There were neon lights overhead, and fans revolved slowly. We were talking about the jungle again when the soup arrived. The waiter ladled it out, *muy picante,* into extra-large bowls that held the innumerable red shellfish as well. While we waited for it to cool off, Paul ordered a jug of fresh beer.

"A pistol is being sent to me. I think I'll take it along just in case."

"The first time I went into the jungle I carried a pistol. I spent most of my time cleaning the thing and never fired it once."

"Why not?"

"There's nothing to shoot at. When those areas were opened up everybody went in with a gun. They shot down everything that moved."

"Still, you never know when a gun might come in handy."

The waiter brought the beer.

"Take a jackknife instead."

We finished the soup and walked around Callao for a while. It's a dirty town with the usual customs buildings and narrow streets all run through with tram tracks. We came upon a small triangular park near the waterfront. Slender palm trees grew above old Spanish cannon along the sea wall. Through the mist and spray thrown up by the waves the black outline of San Lorenzo Island was visible. There's a prison out there. Paul said he came down to Callao often to eat and have a swim at a rowing club to which he belonged.

On the way back to Lima we got stuck behind a tram on Colmena. I told Paul I'd read somewhere that these trams were taken directly from the old Third Avenue Elevated in New York. He laughed and said he'd never heard that before.

■ ■ ■

Rodrigo makes beds at the pensión. He is short and wiry. I always have a feeling that he's going to play a trick on me.

Every day he wears a blue baseball cap pushed back on his forehead, so the long visor sticks up nearly perpendicularly. In the morning he taps softly on my door with his broom handle and whispers in his squeaky voice, *"Señor, son las ocho."*

I get up, dress, and grope wearily in the fog among dovecotes and rabbit warrens to the bathroom on the roof. On the way back I generally find him down on his hands and knees looking for eggs among the boxes and cages. The chickens run free. Sometimes as I go by he holds up an egg and grins.

"Rodrigo, are those good eggs?"

"Si, señor. Very good, very fresh." He showed me a handful. "But very small."

"Where can I find large ones?" I was thinking of keeping some boiled eggs in my room to eat with salt and pepper when I came home from work.

"Ah, *señor,* I know the place. A man has many large brown chickens, all the same colour, from North America. They give very large eggs."

"Much larger than these?"

"The biggest in Lima, also brown. I'll take you to him."

"All right, Rodrigo, one day we'll go together."

My next free day we walked through the city and crossed the Rimac by the bridge near Acho bull ring. A great number of Indians, mostly women and their children, were sitting along the curb. Vendors went among them selling bright-coloured candles. Food stands had been set up at either end of the bridge; *anticuchos* were already roasting on spits. Rodrigo explained that a procession was to pass along this way soon. If we hurried back, we might be able to see it.

The egg man kept an impressive flock of reddish chickens in a whitewashed adobe courtyard. These chickens, he explained, ate a special egg-producing mixture, also prepared in North America. The eggs were extremely large and brown. As he carefully placed a dozen in a paper bag, he whispered to me, "Whenever you desire more eggs, *señor,* just tell Rodrigo here. He shall bring them to you."

"*Sí.* I pass by here every morning on the way to the pensión."

"All right, Rodrigo."

"*Sí, señor,*" murmured the egg man.

We arrived back at the bridge too late for the procession. Far down the street the painted figure of Christ, framed in gold and by many yellow flowers, swayed above the purple-clad bearers. A band was playing. However, the bridge was still crowded and littered with paper and food. Overhead the pale sun moved through the low shifting overcast.

"*Mira, Rodrigo, el sol.*"

"*Sí.*"

I went over to an *anticucho* stand and bought two sticks of roasted heart pieces. I was about to dip mine into a bowl of green pepper sauce when I felt something hard strike me between the shoulder blades. Turning around I saw an old woman in a black shawl standing there with one shoe missing. She was talking to herself in a low harsh monotone. Then the pitch of her voice rose until she was screaming at me in a language I couldn't understand.

"Rodrigo, what did she do that for?"

"She's crazy, *señor,* just a crazy old woman."

She was now waving her arms wildly about. Rodrigo yelled back at her. A crowd gathered, impassive, just looking.

"Perhaps I bumped into her by mistake, or stepped on her toe."

"No, she's just crazy, *señor.*"

"What's she saying?"

Without replying Rodrigo picked up the shoe from the pavement and hurled it back at her. But he threw too high, and it went over her head, over the railing, and down into the river. We all ran to the edge and looked down. The river was only a few feet wide and the shoe lay among the garbage heaps on the bank, an old woman's shoe. The crowd of Indians made no noise, just stared down. The old woman squeezed through and grasped the railing with both hands. I noticed vitiligo on her wrists and neck. She turned and stared up at me with watery eyes, red in the corners. She still looked wild but wasn't saying anything.

"Why did you do that?"

She started shouting again. Rodrigo was dragging at my arm.

"Come on, *señor,* don't talk to her. Let's go."

I released my grip on the rail and pushed through the crowd behind Rodrigo. When we were free I stopped to look back for her. She was not in sight. The old woman had succeeded in making me feel thoroughly uncomfortable.

"Why do you think she threw that shoe, Rodrigo?"

He shrugged his shoulders. "She's a crazy old woman."

"Do you know what she was saying?"

"*No, señor.* She was speaking one of those mountain languages."

We were walking fast now, down the street the procession had taken. I could hear the faint sound of trumpets and drums.

"What about her shoe?"

"*Qué?*"

"Who's going to get the shoe for her?"

"Ah! She can get it herself. Or one of the boys will climb down for it."

We turned down Ucayali. Another crowd had assembled in the square before San Pedro Church.

"The procession must have entered here."

"*Sí.*"

We waited but there was nothing to see from outside the church. A bell tinkled and the people on the steps went down on their knees. Rodrigo was still eating his *anticuchos* and looking around. After a few minutes we continued walking swiftly towards Carabaya.

"*Señor,* I've seen plenty of women like that—all crazy. Whatever they say—it makes no sense."

Back on Carabaya I felt a little easier.

"Rodrigo, have you got those eggs?"

"*Sí, señor.*"

■   ■   ■

I met Anne at 6 a.m. at Parque Universitario, the point of departure for buses, taxis, and *colectivos* leaving the capital for places and towns all over the country. The destinations are usually lettered in white paint on the windshields of the vehicles. But if any question arises, someone is always on hand hoarsely sounding it out. Many of these buses are brightly painted and have names. Ours was *La Estrella del Norte.* I threw our packs up on top and went with Anne to get some coffee.

"How many hours will this be?" I asked her.

"About six or seven."

A few minutes later we were on our way out of the city. I like travelling by bus or any public overland transport. On a slow bus time does not interfere. You just know you're going to get there. I pushed my poncho up against the window and slept. When I awoke we were out in the desert.

"Anne, how do we know where to get off?"

"I don't know. It's just one valley among hundreds."

"Well, we better find out."

"The driver said he'd heard of it."

"I hope he knows what he's talking about. This country all looks the same to me."

I caught the driver's eye in the glass. He smiled and nodded confidently.

The sun shone down and the land threw back the heat. The

road ran monotonously on by the edge of the sea with the same brown hills to the east. I didn't know where we were. The temperature inside the bus increased and some Indians were sick. I dozed off again but opened my eyes from time to time, hoping to locate that stretch of road where the accident had occurred. Often I wondered what happened to those pigs, whether they had dehydrated and died, or were rescued.

Towards the middle of the afternoon the bus stopped and the driver turned around in his seat, grinning at us. "*Aquí estamos.*"

"*Aquí?*"

"*Sí, señorita.*"

He pointed out the window. A dirt track led off across the desert toward the hills. We got down with our packs and the bus went very slowly off. I looked up and down the road and watched the bus grow smaller, twist in the heat distortions, and disappear. Then all the shimmering silence was concentrated on ourselves.

"I hope he knew what he was talking about."

"Here's the track, Caffery."

"There must be dozens of valleys up among those hills. How do we know which one is ours?"

"This track is supposed to lead to it."

"You're not worried, are you?"

"No, what's there to worry about?"

"Nothing. The track looks used. Let's go."

I let her walk ahead and we proceeded in silence. There is nothing to say out there in the desert. The ground was flat and stony, with a few dry stream beds. Water must flow through here sometime. After an hour we slung down our packs and had a drink.

"How far?"

"About ten miles."

The road gradually lifted out of the desert plain. Before it wound around behind the first hill we looked back and had a good view of land and sea. The lowering sun cast shadows from the large sand dunes on the beach. Then the sea was lost from sight. Gray cacti grew on the hillsides, among boulders.

"At least something grows up here."

Anne did not seem to hear. The back of her shirt was wet around the pack.

As we progressed more signs of vegetation appeared: grass by the side of the road and shrubs up among the boulders.

"Anne, I thought you said this was the driest valley in Peru. What's all this grass?"

"I don't know, Caffery. Perhaps we've taken the wrong road."

"It leads somewhere, that's for certain. I've seen tire tracks in the lee of some of these boulders."

We stopped and rested once more, sitting on some stones that had rolled out onto the road. I lit a cigarette and shook a pebble out of my shoe. In the silence I heard the sound of an engine.

"Someone's coming."

An automobile was being driven very fast over the rough road, raising a great plume of dust. It disappeared around a rock outcropping then came on again and drew up before us. A man in a wide brown hat got out, took a look at us sitting on the rocks, and asked where we were going. He spoke in English.

"Valle de las Culebras," I said.

He informed us that we were on the wrong road. The Valle de las Culebras was more than twenty kilometers away to the north. "But it's too late to go there today. You may spend tonight on my farm, and I shall take you there in the morning."

"Do you have a farm near here?"

"Yes."

"I thought all this land was desert."

"You shall see."

We rolled the boulders out of the way, got into the old car, and drove off. The man introduced himself as Señor Alvarado.

"Why are you going to the Valle de las Culebras? Looking for *huacos?*"

"Yes."

"I believe a group was in there a few months ago. I suppose they must have taken nearly everything."

"We make a search for anything they have overlooked. Generally they make only a superficial examination of the graves they have opened, looking for gold and silver."

"We didn't even bring a shovel," I said.

"I see."

We drove on for several miles among gray hills that grew steeper and rockier. Evidence of landslide was common. At last we came out at the bottom of a long narrow valley that sloped upward between two spurs of mountains. This valley was cultivated right up to the rock escarpments on either side. Out in the middle two enormous pines rose above lesser trees, between which the white walls of a house reflected the late afternoon sun. After so much desolation I could hardly believe what I was looking at.

"How can this valley exist?"

"A small river flows down out of the mountains."

"What grows here?"

"Mostly cotton and grapes, but I have attempted to diversify the crops recently and have planted some apples and avocado trees."

"Do apples grow well in this dry country?"

"Yes. We have imported a special variety from Australia— called Tropical Beauties."

"I love avocados."

"They do very well here. Some grow to be the size of small melons."

We passed a stand of eucalyptus. Sr. Alvarado explained that wood was scarce and expensive.

"Look at the size of those pine trees."

"They were planted two hundred years ago to mark the house for travellers such as yourselves. It's a very old farm."

Sr. Alvarado had just driven up from Lima. He was a modest man but one could see that he was proud of his farm. I liked to hear him talk about it. A servant came out to meet the car, and Sr. Alvarado showed us some rooms in a guest house.

"You must be tired from your long walk and would like to take a siesta. Please come to the house when you are rested. My family is in Lima; it will be a pleasure for me to have company."

I lay down on the bed and fell asleep almost immediately. Anne was still sleeping when I awoke an hour later, so I quietly put on my boots and slipped out of the house just as the sun was going down behind the ridge. I wandered around, took a look at the fighting cocks kept apart in separate cages. Blue peacocks were strutting about. Water flowed in irrigation ditches among the fruit trees. It was a cool, quiet place. Walking away from the house, I crossed a dusty soccer field where barefoot Indians were kicking a ball around. At the end of the field I stopped and looked up the narrow valley to where the fields of cotton and grapes extended to the base of the eroded mountains. I would like to have a farm like this. At least you can see what you've got. A wind was rising now as the temperature dropped, picking up the swirling dust eddies off the field, and I turned back toward the house.

From one side of the field the wind carried voices. I went over and looked down into a hollow. Sr. Alvarado was squatting on his haunches in the dust, talking to a group of Indians. They didn't see me and I couldn't make out all they said, especially the Indians, who spoke in high, difficult voices. The dialogue seemed to be about some projects on the farm. Soon it became so dark that all that remained visible were Sr. Alvarado's white shirt, the shapes of the Indians squatting on the ground, and the glow of the cigarettes. When I went away the wind still bore the sound of Sr. Alvarado's voice and the Indians' coughing and spitting.

That evening Sr. Alvarado mixed up some pisco sours with his own pisco made right on the hacienda. I told him what I had overheard.

"Every week we talk like that. We start off with the farm and move on to politics—always politics."

"What do they want to know about?"

"What's going on outside the farm. They're like any country people. Nobody ever tells them anything. So I tell them, the good and the bad, land reform and the trouble up in the Sierra. I like to talk and so do they. I look forward to it. This afternoon I was driving very fast—I was afraid I would be late for them."

Sr. Alvarado seemed such a gentle man, of such civility, that I took a strong liking to him. I never saw a man so at ease. Later on he went on to tell us about pecans and olives and mangoes. His talk made me want to have a farm of my own.

I went to bed right after dinner, thinking that this would be the last good sleep I would get for a few nights. Tomorrow we would be out in that dry valley, lying on rocks and gravel. For several hours I slept soundly, a deep sleep in the dry night air of the desert, when suddenly I opened my eyes and was wide awake. Something was happening; I was trembling all over. Then a peacock let out a long terrible screech, followed by a distant rumbling somewhere up in the Andes. I sat rigidly upright in the bed. All the hair on my head and on the back of my neck bristled like a mad dog's.

"Anne, are you awake?"

"Yes." Her voice came out of the blackness.

"What was that?"

"I don't know. A landslide, I think."

"Did you hear that peacock?"

"Yes."

"Anne, my hair is standing on end. What caused the land-slide?"

"An earth tremor must have set it off."

"I was scared. I'm still stiff."

"I know, Caffery. What time is it?"

I looked at the luminous watch face. "Three o'clock exactly."

"Are you all right, Caffery?"

"I'm all right. Those peacocks make an awful noise."

For the rest of the night I remained locked in that peacock shriek and mountain rumbling and could not sleep.

In the morning Sr. Alvarado drove us back to the highway, then for miles up another dirt track. There he stopped the car, opened the glove compartment, and took out a bottle of his pisco. "This will keep you warm after the sun goes down."

We said goodbye and started off across the stony plain. The land, reddish now, was more desolate than ever. I saw no vegetation, no cover anywhere. Beyond, range on range of hills and ridges lifted into the heated silence. Anne walked ahead, her shoes raising a motionless pall of dust between us. I kept my eye out for snakes. It would be bad luck to get bitten out here.

The plain was broken by a long sloping ridge. We went left and trudged out into a vast cul-de-sac rimmed by rocky mountain crests that rose as steeply as cliffs.

"Why this is called a valley I don't know. It's nothing more than a dead-end canyon." My voice echoed faintly.

We went on a little farther.

"Anne, say something."

"Nothing has changed in this valley for five hundred years."

"Why?"

"There is no wind and no rain. Nothing to cause erosion."

We crossed a dry sandy stream bed.

"This dried up hundreds of years ago. For lack of water the

village had already been deserted by the time of the Conquest."

"I don't know why anybody would want to live out here anyhow. It's too hot, and there's no shade."

"When the stream flowed, the valley was green."

"It didn't last."

We came to the remains of a pre-Inca village. It consisted of thousands of red stones strewn out over the plain. In some instances even the shapes of foundations were evident. On a slight rising to one side of the village white bones and skulls were scattered, reflecting the sunlight. We threw down our packs and made an inspection of the burial ground. About fifty or sixty graves had been excavated in a haphazard fashion. Shards, lengths of matted brown cloth, and bits of wood were intermingled with the whitened bones and skulls, to which layers of the desiccated flesh and the long hair still clung. We examined a few open graves. They exuded the usual musty smell of death.

While Anne patiently searched for bits of coloured cloth and patterned shards I looked among the bones. Some of these people had red hair, probably dyed. Their teeth were in excellent condition; I didn't see any cavities. A few skulls had russet scorpions living inside. But many of the skulls were broken. I kicked them aside, and they went rattling down the hill. The scorpions scurried away.

"Whoever came through here made a mess. Everything seems to be smashed."

"Looking for gold and silver," she said. "That's all they want."

"I wonder if they found any."

"If those grave robbers hadn't been so careless, some of these mummies would have been in good condition. Look at this."

She showed me the perfectly preserved foot of a baby, with the flesh and miniature toenails.

"I see an owl."

A small owl was perched on a rock. Several others flitted silently among the graves. Yellow lizards hid in the sand.

Anne called me over. She had uncovered the entire upper portion of a man. The flesh was hard and dry. You could see the lips, the tendons in the neck, the nipples on the chest.

"How are they preserved like this?" I asked.

"The corpse is disemboweled and placed in the sun until all liquid has evaporated, then drawn up into a foetal position, wrapped, and entombed."

"The body must be stiff after exposure to the sun. How do they pull it into foetal position, crack its joints?"

"I don't know; I suppose they do that first."

"Crack its joints?"

"No, draw it up into foetal pose. The dry desert air and soil preserves them."

We scratched around for a couple of hours without finding anything of importance. Anne showed me a shard inscribed with coiled snakes.

"This valley got its name from the numbers of *huacos* with snakes on them found here."

"There must be thousands of them."

"Thousands of what?"

"Snakes."

"I don't think so. There aren't many snakes on the coast. Snakeskins brought from the jungle must have inspired them, or just tales of snakes."

The sun had heated up the land so I could feel it through my boots. We returned to where we had dropped our packs. While Anne prepared something to eat I rigged up a blanket with sticks and rocks so we could at least have a little protection. As we ate, the heat and silence began to close in once more, and I found myself whistling. I never saw such a barren land: now the reddish canyon lurched with a false sense of life. The only real living things were ourselves, encamped at the bottom of this enormous basin, and the owls and scorpions and lizards.

After lunch we lay in the shade of the blanket. I blinked my eyes in the glare and managed to fall asleep. About five o'clock the heat began to abate. Anne said she wanted to investigate the other side of the valley, where some mounds indicated another burial site. I let her go off by herself. I decided to scale the valley wall and get a better view.

The climbing was not easy. The rocks came away when I gripped them for support. Lizards were more numerous, basking on stones, and once I thought I saw a snake slide out of sight. About halfway up I came to a level place covered by flat stones that had been worked by hand. Among the rocks there were sea shells. I noticed that a corner of blue sea was visible from this spot, which must have something to do with the presence of these shells. Probably those Incas sat up here eating clams while gazing at the sea.

About a mile away on the other side of the valley Anne was poking around among the graves. I shouted at her, but the sound died away in the silence. Perhaps she had found something. I went down and started to cross the valley floor. She was standing on a burial mound and waving at me. I ran over to her.

"I've found a broken shovel, Caffery, and have begun to dig into an unopened grave. It's lined with stone. We might find something."

She led me to the place. I picked up the shovel and began to dig as Anne pulled the rocks aside. Soon I hit something and dug around it. Anne was down on her knees, clearing the dust away with her hands from the wrappings of a mummy. I dug some more until I was able to get underneath and lift it out, placing it upright on the ground. It was a pod-shaped thing, a dull cone less than three feet high, heavily wrapped in brown cloth. It seemed small to me, but I suppose these bodies must shrink considerably when placed out to dry in the sun.

"Now what are we going to do with it?"

"Open it up."

I took out my knife and began to cut away the wrappings, one at a time at first, but in great stabs and slices when I discovered their thickness.

"Be careful. You'll injure the mummy."

As I worked from the top, the head was first disclosed.

"Look at it."

The head was tilted back and the mouth stretched wide open, howling, at the hour of death, like a dog at the moon. Long thin fingers, with the dry flesh and perfect fingernails, pressed against the cheekbones.

"A woman."

"Look at her hair."

The long red hair was still perfectly braided.

"Anne, let's leave her alone."

"No. Open it up, Caffery. We've come this far."

"She smells bad, Anne."

I stripped away the remaining mass of crumbling wrappings, darker on the inside. The knees were drawn up tightly against the stomach and chest. In the woman's belly lay another smaller skeleton, also in the same foetal position.

"Look at that."

"She died in childbirth."

"Was it born?"

"I think so, born dead."

I stood up. Although the sky was still bright, little light was left in the canyon. No wind. No sound.

"Anne, I've had enough of this. Let's find ourselves a place to sleep."

"Right here would be good. The ground is sandy."

"No, I'm not going to sleep in this cemetery."

"Enough bits of wood are lying about that we could have a fire."

"Too many scorpions around."

"There are scorpions everywhere."

"Besides, it's too close to the side of the mountain. Any earth tremor would bury us in a landslide. Let's move right out onto the canyon floor, where we put our packs down this morning."

Night fell quickly, but I had enough time to collect some ancient sticks for a fire, over which Anne heated up some cans of bully beef, as she called it. I was looking forward to that bottle of pisco. After dinner we sat by the fire and smoked cigarettes and drank it down. It was about the smoothest I ever tasted and, out on the floor of that canyon, just what we needed.

Before long we had to put on our ponchos.

"Caffery, are you happy we came out here?"

"Yes, but I wouldn't want to be in this canyon by myself."

"It's a pretty wild place."

"Nobody ever wants to come alone into a canyon like this. If I were out here by myself, I'd be hugging my knees and whistling, playing the flashlight around the camp."

"With you I don't mind it."

"Let's leave tomorrow. We can go down and sleep near the ocean. I had a view of it from the mountain."

"All right."

Anne began to put the food cans into the pack.

"Anne, did that peacock scare you last night?"

"No, natural things don't frighten me."

"I didn't shut my eyes for the rest of the night."

"What frightens me is stupidity."

"Like the pig accident."

"It's so unnecessary. David was killed because he wasn't paying attention. His mind was on the view."

"But when the mountains start moving there's not much you can do."

"The mountain didn't push him. He put his foot down in the wrong place and slipped. He didn't have to die."

We had some more pisco. The fire began to die down, as I couldn't find any more wood, so we fixed up a place to sleep.

The ground was like stone, but we had brought plenty of blankets and were able to make a fairly comfortable bed. I managed to get a few hours' rest.

The next morning we hoisted up our packs and walked out of that canyon. It was a good fifteen miles back to the highway and the sun was right over our heads. Soon we came to a track.

"There are roads all over the place. Where do they go?"

"I don't know."

Before long a bus came down out of the hills and stopped for us. It was full of Indians, but they let us climb up on top among the bundles and crates.

"Where do these buses come from?"

"Don't know!"

I was beginning to enjoy the breeze when it blew my straw hat off. It landed back on the road.

"My hat!"

"Sombrero!"

"Sombrero! Stop the bus!"

The driver stopped. I climbed down and ran back to pick up the hat. By noon we were down on the beach and in the water. It was a great relief to be out of the canyon. I understood why the Incas took the trouble to climb that steep cliff in order to have a view of the sea. In the afternoon we had a siesta on the warm sand. As the sun dropped toward the horizon I took a walk up the shore. Hundreds of red crabs live on this beach, scurrying back and forth between their holes in the sand. I found a rusty piece of old bucket and tried to catch some. You have to race around and grab them before they dive into their holes, or dig madly before they go too deep. I managed to capture about twenty in this manner.

When I returned Anne said, "Caffery, you've got nice legs."

I showed her the crabs.

"They're inedible."

I dumped the crabs out and they ran off in all directions

across the sand. For dinner we had more of the same bully beef and a few other things out of cans. However, there was plenty of driftwood for a good fire and I scooped out a camp among the sand dunes. The beach is very wide at this point. We finished off the last of the pisco and made our beds in the sand.

"Put your hand into the sand, Anne. You can still feel the heat of the day."

"The sun was hot."

"But I'm afraid it's going to be a damp night. There's always dampness near the sea, even in a desert."

"We have enough blankets. These high dunes should protect us from the wind."

"Anne, what was the matter with those crabs?"

"They give you stomach cramps."

I drew the blanket over us. "Who's looking after Jason?"

"That Indian girl you saw. I'm not worried. He's a boy. I'm glad he's a boy."

"I agree."

"I like to think of the possibilities for his life. It will be easier for him."

"Than for you?"

"Yes. A man can more easily lead a life without the usual supports."

"I think so."

"I want to be with him until he's ready for school. Otherwise I'd go off somewhere, travelling alone."

"Where?"

"Anywhere."

"Like Bonsal. He always travels alone."

"Yes, like him. Perhaps I'll take Jason and do it anyway. I loathe teaching and I don't feel that I can bluff my way through another year of it."

"It's not a bad life."

"I didn't ask for it."

"You attempt to see something in it."

"I have it and must live with it."

Although the sand was more comfortable than the canyon floor, I don't think I closed my eyes once that night. I've never been able to sleep anywhere except in a decent bed, and each recollection I have of a night spent out of doors has been one of sleeplessness and regret. The sand flies bit my ankles and wrists and ears. So the whole night I lay there on my back with my hands behind my head as Anne slept at my side. From time to time she would wake up and ask if I were sleeping, and each time I would answer no. Trucks passed all night along the highway and what with the wind behind them I could hear the sounds of their engines coming down from the north miles away, long before their headlights came into view. After a while I got to listening for those trucks, and to counting them.

The next morning I lost my sheath knife in the sand. We spent the whole day on the beach, swimming and walking up and down and lying in the sun. That totally deserted beach gave us all the space we wanted.

It was nearly dusk as we climbed up the embankment to the highway. The sun was setting and spreading itself out across the horizon, touching with the last of its light the orange hills to the east. The sea was calm, with only a few waves; each dune seemed scooped from the shadow it cast on the sand. As we waited by the side of the road, the sun squared and disappeared into the sea. Not much later the bus came by and we rode the whole night back to Lima.

■ ■ ■

The day of my return I went around to see Sra. Davis. It was in the late afternoon. She lives at the bottom of a quiet street near the river, where children squat on the pavement, playing their games. Often in that neighborhood I hear the knife sharpener raising his four-noted whistle to the open windows above the street. I believe that old women must sit there, slightly recessed in the shadows of their rooms, unmoving and looking down.

Sra. Davis brought out a *tapa* and a bottle of beer and listened to me talk about the trip. Some reproductions of French Impressionists hung on the walls, and one portrait of herself twenty years younger. There was nothing sloppy about the way in which she lived. She owned few possessions but knew where they all were.

I told her I had left the *chorizo* behind in a bookshop on Unión.

"Did you return for it?"

"Two days later. The woman had found it but she'd given it away to that French boy who works there, the one with glasses."

"No, I don't believe it. She gave it away?"

"She didn't know whom it belonged to."

"What if I forget my sweater there while I'm looking at books? Is she going to give it to the shopgirl to take home?"

"She thought it would spoil."

"In the poor Indian shops off in the *callejones* they hide anything you forget and deny you left it there, but not on Jirón de la Unión!"

"Jean-Paul is quite poor. I don't think he has much to eat. He took the *chorizo* home, and he and his wife ate it the same night."

"He ate it all? It was a very large *chorizo*—more than one kilo."

"I don't think he'd ever seen a *chorizo* before, probably thought it was some kind of French sausage. Anyway, he told me that he had never tasted anything better. Ate it all in one sitting."

"*Pobrecito.* The whole *chorizo.*"

"The woman was very sorry. She said she didn't think it would keep."

"They last for months."

"She'd never seen a *chorizo* before either, and knew nothing about them."

"But in a first-class shop like that, on Jirón de la Unión. If I happen to forget my pocketbook there, what will happen? She'll give it away."

"No. She just didn't know what to do with the *chorizo*."

I ate the *tapa*—some cold sea bass with a garlic sauce—and lit up a cigarette. Sra. Davis went into the kitchen to get me another beer.

"Señora, I'm getting tired of this heavy mist. My room at the pensión is damp."

"Winter is lasting longer than usual this year. Normally the sun has burned it away by this time."

"I'm planning to take a long trip—over the Sierra and into the Selva."

"When? You're always travelling."

"Soon. Perhaps in a few weeks."

"Solito?"

"Sí."

"You'll cross the Sierra by plane."

"Overland. Otherwise I'll see nothing."

"At this time of year? *Muy frío allí.* Take many clothes."

"I'm travelling light for the Selva."

"I'll knit you a heavy scarf to keep you warm in the mountains."

"Yes?"

"What colour do you want?"

"Green. A long green scarf—two meters."

Back at the pensión Rodrigo informed me that a large procession would be passing along Colmena that night. This seemed to be the season for them. However, I took my time having my shoes shined and arrived too late. The wide avenue had been shut off to traffic and was filled with thousands of people. Military music blared from speakers attached high up on the lamp posts. Children dashed wildly through the crowd. I wandered in the noise and candle smoke until the first automobiles began to push their way through. Just then I caught a glimpse of Bonsal and tried to follow him, but he disappeared among so many people. In a crowd he moves quickly. But a few minutes later I stepped into Rincon Toni's and found him at a table with a beer in front of him. He was dressed in a dark suit.

"Did you see me out there?"

"No."

"I tried to catch up to you, but you were walking too fast."

"Someone was trying to pick my pocket."

"Anyway, I knew you were headed in this direction."

I ordered a beer and a plate of olives.

"I'm glad you found me."

Bonsal announced that he was returning to the United States for a few months and asked if I would like to move into his apartment rent free while he was away. "Well, do you want it?"

"Yes, I do. Very much."

"Then that's settled."

"But I've definitely decided to take a trip as well, into the interior."

"When?"

"Soon. This week I'll ask for a leave of absence from my job."

"Why don't you quit that job? It's no good."

"I know, but how will I live?"

"You can find another way. Involve yourself with the country."

"Perhaps I will."

We crossed town on foot to that restaurant near the railroad station, where we asked for the usual liver and spinach, and a bottle of pisco to wash it down.

"Paul, the revolver I was telling you about has arrived."

"You're going to take it with you?"

"I had such a terrible time getting it out of customs, I'm not leaving it behind."

"It's a mistake."

"They made me go all the way out to Limatambo Airport. I spent the whole afternoon there clearing the thing through customs."

"It's the bureaucrats. They hold everything up."

"Dozens of old men sitting around in rooms with splintered wood floors."

After dinner we walked slowly back across the city towards his apartment. There's a park off Avenida Wilson where we sat down on an old bandstand and smoked. The fog obscured everything but the street lamps.

"Think about Lima when you're in the Selva."

"All right."

"The jungle puts things into focus. The air is good there. If you get on a river look for monkeys."

"I'll bring one back for you."

"I'll be gone when you return."

I was sorry to leave Bonsal. I would be travelling alone in a part of Peru he knew well, while he would be out of the country. I walked back toward Carabaya in the misting night and crossed Plaza San Martín as the last tram rumbled in from Callao. No one was around.

In my room were a small can of oil and a rag. Sitting on the edge of my bed I carefully cleaned and oiled the gun. When all the points of rust were gone and the gun metal shone, I slipped it into the leather holster, strapped it to my hip, and stood before the mirror to see how it looked. It was a heavy revolver but I intended to take it with me no matter what Bonsal said.

ii

The train left at seven o'clock. I arrived early enough to buy some mangoes from an old woman at the gate. The second-class car was already filled with soldiers and Indians, who offered me a seat next to the window. They all had mangoes too, presumably bought from the same old woman. There was a lot of the noise and laughing and excitement that precedes a trip.

As we steamed out everyone was hanging out the windows and waving. Some children ran alongside. Up under the dusty hills were stacked the chaotic tin and wood shack towns, overhung by the haze of early morning cook smoke. I could see some Indians up there stopping whatever they were doing to wave back at the train. In a few more minutes we were out of the city and the passengers sat back to enjoy the trip. I was hungry and took out my knife to peel a mango. It is one of these Swiss army knives, bright red with several shiny instruments besides the blade. It immediately caught the attention of everyone around me. This kind of thing had happened before, so I wasn't surprised. I opened it up and handed it around so the others could have a look. One soldier was particularly interested when I told him that every man in the Swiss army carries one of these knives. I don't know whether this is true or not. When the knife was returned to me I peeled my mango with it; then everyone else peeled his mango with it. Meanwhile the train had crossed the narrow coastal strip and had begun the ascent into the mountains. By the time we broke out of the clouds into the sunlight, all the mangoes had been eaten.

This is supposed to be one of the highest railroads in the world, built by the British at considerable expense and effort. For this purpose I hear they imported large numbers of Chinese labourers, which explains why you see so many of them in Lima. Due to the steep rising terrain we were forced to pass through a number of switchbacks, a tedious process. I slept most of the way.

The train stopped at La Oroya, an Andean mining town at about twelve thousand feet. A cold thin wind was sweeping down from the slate peaks. Waiting for the connecting train to Cerro de Pasco, I leaned on the railing of a bridge over a gorge that divides the town. On one side are the smelting plant and slag heaps, on the other rows and rows of miners' dwellings. The Indian men trot by in ponchos and black knee breeches, the women in felt hats and bright-coloured skirts. A man selling flutes came along. He and his friend played the fragile Indian music for me. You have to be close up to hear it.

The train pulled out and climbed once more until the track levelled out across a vast *altiplano*. It had a smooth texture of green and brown, and the sky was such a dark blue—going on black. Out among the outlines of stone corrals I saw men on foot tending isolated herds of llamas, feeding on bunch grass. Glittering silver peaks of the Cordilleras rise in the distance. There is great space here over the land.

The Indians with whom I was now riding were a dirty, rough-skinned lot, with running sores and giving off that musty smell of their clothes and towns. A man in back had got hold of a bottle of beer, howled and laughed for a while, but now lay dead drunk and sick under the wooden bench, the face stone-like. The other passengers, mostly women with sucking babies, were all chewing on some nuts and spitting the shells out onto the floor. I wrapped my new scarf and poncho around me, but still I felt cold and uncomfortable. The high altitude was giving me a headache. Therefore I paid the conductor an extra supplement on the ticket and moved into the first-class car, where I was the only passenger. They served me a meal, which I ate absent-mindedly while gazing out the window.

The train made several stops at villages along the way. Sheep carcasses hang out in the sun. Women besiege the train with steaming bowls of tripe and the opaque *chicha* beer foaming out of earthen jugs. I got down once, bought a *pastel de choclo* that had no raisins and no meat, and walked out onto the *altiplano*. Two large black birds were sitting on the ground, grunting to each other. They flew heavily off at my approach. The high-altitude wind blows in steadily from the plain, whipping up the ponchos of the Indians squatting in the lee of a mud wall. I felt a little dizzy climbing back onto the train.

Cerro de Pasco is another large mining town at fourteen thousand feet. I was able to find a reasonable room in a hotel run by the company. In the fireplace some logs smouldered. I attempted to stir them up, to get some heat out of them, but at this altitude not enough air exists for a real blaze. My headache had become worse, so I took some aspirin and lay down on the bed, drawing the coarse brown poncho over me. But the dull cold entered my body. I gave that up and left the hotel to walk and warm myself. The sun was lowering toward the bleak horizon. At a great height in the sky some huge birds could be seen—probably condors.

You can hear the sound of the mines in the distance. Heavy structured machinery on the hill is precisely delineated against a clear metallic sky. As whistles blow in the fading light the Indians stream back from the mines. You see them pass silent and sullen, their boots crunching on gravel. Every other one seems to have one leg shorter than the other or some awful skin disease. The sun sets colourless over the mass of tin dwellings spread out across the plain.

At the bottom of the main street a bus was loading. I made for it. A man on top was hoisting up bundles and suitcases and securing them with a net. I shouted at him.

"Dónde va, hombre, dónde va?"

"Huánuco, hombre, Huánuco."

I was up that bus and had my money out so fast he didn't know where it came from. I didn't worry about the change, either. The bus was leaving in ten minutes and I had the ticket in my pocket. I went back up that hill as fast as possible. Entering the hotel I yelled at the Indian behind the desk that I was leaving town. On the way out the door I tossed him the key. He took one step forward, caught the key, and watched me go by, the mouth gaping. The bus didn't leave for another half hour, but I found my seat and stayed where I was.

We headed out over the *altiplano,* this time in darkness. The road was rough but level. Only when another truck or bus passed did you realize how dusty it was. Seated up behind the driver I was able to see headlights approaching over the plain a good twenty minutes before we met the vehicle. The road ascended again. The night cold was intense. At last the descent down the eastern side of the Andes was begun. The road wound down through increasingly warmer and denser layers of air. Poplars and eucalyptus grew along the roadside. White water foamed over boulders in the moonlight. The night air became so warm that I opened the window and stuck my elbow out. I felt grateful for the possibility of movement.

The next day I was on a different bus out of Huánuco climbing through red and brown hills, with patches of green where they have been terraced and cultivated. Mostly potatoes grow here. Then after many hours, we traversed a ridge and descended through vegetation that had suddenly turned tropical.

The road became rutted and puddled as the forest rose and closed in. I found myself looking back at the dry hills that still remained in view. Ahead the land lay blue and green, unbroken in hazy vegetation.

After one has lived in Lima and has passed through the Sierra, coming down upon the jungle bears a form of unreality. But in face of the contrast there remains a connection. When I try to link these topographical units I know that the sad haze of blue is everywhere the same. It is true that the hills of Tingo Maria will be blue, but only a more abandoned expression of a constant backdrop. After all, if I looked far enough, the slate quality of the Pacific turned into azure water lanes, and in the Sierra there is only the sky. Now, foothills go from purple into blue, shadings perhaps speaking of a common reality.

At three o'clock the bus halted on the side of a hill where water from a spring flowed down across the road. Whoever says that jungle water is not fit to drink is mistaken: that was some of the coldest water I have ever tasted. At four o'clock a thunderstorm broke over us, leaving the air clean and cool afterwards. By nightfall we were in Tingo Maria.

All I could make out was one long dusty main street lined on either side by low-silhouette general stores, storage sheds, and fresh-orange-juice stands. Trucks and trucks converted into buses roared up and down, raising the light dust into the warm night air. Loudspeakers attached to lamp posts let out some fast Cuban music. Insects swarm through the light. In a playground at one end of the street a man was carefully cutting the grass with a machete.

I carried my bag into a bar and sat down. This bar also served as entrance to an adjacent movie theatre. Several Europeans in wide straw hats were waiting to enter. They looked like farmers to me. I overheard them speaking Italian, Spanish, English and some other language that sounded like Polish or Russian. Some argument was going on.

"*Por Dios,* Giovanni. Give me the money. Five *soles!*" The tall balding one was pleading as the others bought tickets.

"No, Sàndor, goddammit! You borrow too much money, you put gasoline from my tank into your car. You're fat from my food. This time, nothing!" returned the shorter one with the dirty straw hat moulded into some Alpine shape.

"Please, Giovanni! *Cinco soles!*"

"Go home, Sàndor. I'll see you tomorrow."

"Giovanni!"

"Go home!"

"Giovanni, I can't. I have only one litre of gasoline in my car."

"Then walk home."

"Giovanni, *por favor!*"

"Jesus Christ. I'll meet you here after the cinema and buy you some gasoline."

"Giovanni, give me the money now."

"No, you'll spend it on the cinema."

"Yes, I want to go to the cinema. What else can I do with five *soles?* Please, Giovanni."

"No!"

The short one disappeared into the theatre after his friends. The other gave me an exasperated glance, sat down, and began to drum his fingers on the table, muttering something in that eastern European language. When the waiter came and I asked him how to get to the hotel, the man leapt up from his chair.

"You want to go to the hotel? I'll take you!" he exclaimed.

A minute later we were in his Land Rover driving out of town. The hotel, a long, low construction of unpainted wood with wide verandas and screened porches, is located about a mile away on the river. Sàndor came in with me. We had a couple of drinks in the bar and talked about Tingo Maria.

"This is high jungle here, *La Montaña.* The air is cool at night."

"I suppose one can sleep well here."

He asked me what I was doing in Tingo Maria. I told him I was just travelling through.

"I've been here five years."

"You must like it."

"Farming is dull, farming communities are dull. I travel down to Lima occasionally, but never for long."

"I found that an exhausting trip overland."

"But after a few days in Lima I become anxious to return."

"Those Sierra towns are awful places. The wind continually blowing and the mountain sickness—I couldn't stand it."

"I'm always glad to come back to Tingo Maria."

"What grows around here?"

"Coffee mostly."

"Does coffee grow well in this tropical country?"

"No. The finest coffee is grown at higher altitudes. Besides, the soil here is too acid to carry on agriculture. It wears out after a few years. The plant diseases and destructive insects are too numerous to combat. However, I find the climate extremely pleasant."

"If the land's no good, why do people grow coffee on it?"

"Because Tingo Maria is such an agreeable place to live."

"Can you make any money?"

"You heard my argument with Giovanni, no? I don't have five *soles* and he wouldn't lend me five *soles*. Why should he? I've borrowed thousands from him already, and millions from the bank."

"Do you have a coffee plantation?"

"I do, yes."

"Don't you have any income at all from the coffee?"

"Do you want to see my farm? Come to my house tonight, and you can look at my coffee trees in the morning."

"Do you mean it?"

"Of course. It's not far."

"I'll buy the gasoline."

"Five litres only!"

"All right."

Now, I thought, this is an opportunity to see something of the jungle and how people live out there.

I paid up and put my bag into the Land Rover again, and we drove back into town to a place where they sell gasoline. A man came out of a shed and pumped it by hand from a fifty-gallon drum.

"Fill it up, please," I told him.

"No, five litres only, I said!"

"You have to bring me back."

"Five litres is enough for a round trip."

"Can't we drive around some when we get out there?"

"I live at the end of the road. There's no place to go except on foot."

"I'd like to see some of the land."

"We can pay Giovanni a visit, but five litres is still sufficient!"

While we were arguing the man went on pumping. When Sàndor finally stopped him the tank was nearly full. Insects were swarming all over the headlights of the Land Rover.

■　■　■

I awoke and looked out through the open window at the massive trees that grew at the edge of the cleared land. The upper branches are heavily festooned with white lianas that hang motionless against the shadow of the forest. Sàndor was out there among the stumps and banana trees, his hands on his hips, looking down at a low platform of palm thatching. When I called to him he turned and beckoned me to come outside.

"I hope you slept well."

"I did."

"These are my coffee trees you're looking at."

"What?"

I could see something green beneath the loose thatching but I had to get down on my hands and knees to have a better look.

"Pretty small."

"Just seedlings."

"Why do you have them covered up like that?"

"To protect them from the sun. They're still quite delicate."

"When will they begin producing coffee?"

"In five or six years' time. You see what farming amounts to—waiting for the plants to grow."

"Can you wait that long?"

"I don't know."

"What else do you do out here—besides wait?"

"I work on my house."

In the middle of this rough open space cut from the jungle stood a small brick house with a tin roof. Here Sàndor lived with a Hungarian manservant named Vasil, who had opened the door for us last night and then disappeared back into the kitchen. He looked wild-eyed and uncertain to me.

We went back inside. Vasil served us breakfast of papaya and coffee.

"You built this house yourself?"

"I did, yes."

"How long did it take you?"

"Three years. I put all my capital into it, with just enough money left over to buy the seedlings. I can't live here without a house."

After breakfast he showed me around. There were photographs of castles and forest hunting scenes. Sàndor explained that the whole family had been driven out of Hungary during the war, and now it was impossible to return. Everything had been confiscated or destroyed. Only the photographs remained.

"Caffery, this morning I must go and oversee some work that's being done."

"I'd like to come along."

"It's not far. Afterwards I'll take you to a special place I know about."

We went down through the banana grove. I heard the sound of machetes up ahead and we came to the edge of the forest, where men were attempting to clear the land. A great wreckage of fallen trees covered the ground. At our appearance the men, barefoot Indians in old straw hats and open shirts, stopped work. While Sàndor talked to them I sat down on a log. They had chopped down some big trees with those machetes. The trunks were lichen-covered and gripped by thick vines. The branches were gnarled as if from grappling with other trees.

When Sàndor finished we walked down to the river. It was about fifty yards wide at this point and running fast. We stepped into the warm swirling water and almost at once it was waist deep. While Sàndor surged easily through the stiff current I floundered behind in great difficulty to keep myself from being swept away downstream. At last I clambered up the far bank twenty yards below him. We kept on, following a dry sandy stream bed back into the forest. The glare of sun off the cracked mud and crisscross of fallen tree trunks was so bright that my eyes naturally sought the shadows of the jungle. Here the going was easier except when we had to climb among the dead logs and spectral branches.

After a mile of this we entered the undergrowth and wound among a great density of trees. The light was cut off by the foliage over our heads. It's impossible to determine the height of these trees, which simply disappear into the vegetation above. However, judging by their girths and the size of the roots, they must be enormous. I stumbled heavily along behind Sàndor.

Finally we emerged into another clearing, this one completely overgrown. I blinked into the sunlight. All was silent except for the high shrill of insects. Along the edge of the trees stood a row of open sheds with caving tin roofs and rotten beams.

"What's all this?"

"There used to be a lumbering operation here."

Under the sheds were all kinds of heavy machinery, being rusted away. Creepers spiraled around gearshifts and hydraulic systems. Tall grass grew up between tractor treads and links of heavy chain. Rubber tires had cracked and split in the heat. It was a place where snakes and small animals hid.

"What happened to it?"

"It went broke."

"Why? There are plenty of trees around here."

"To get at the one hardwood you want you have to cut down twenty others."

"Still, lumbering must be a good business. You chop down the trees, saw them up, and ship them out."

"I've thought about it myself. But the cost of transport to the coast is too high. It's cheaper to import the wood from Canada."

"I never saw so many trees. There must be some way of making the operation profitable. Have your own fleet of trucks."

"That's expensive."

Sàndor led me across to the other side of the clearing where a stream came rambling down through a gorge in the hills. The water was as clear and pure as any mountain stream.

"Here it is."

We scrambled upstream over smooth rocks, plunged with all our clothes on into deep pools, and climbed through waterfalls. Finally we just took our clothes off and threw them down on the rocks. As we climbed, the gorge became narrower. A web of creepers and flowers clung to the cliffs' sides. Light green lianas hung down from the trees along the top of the gorge, trembling if they touched a waterfall. On a flat stone where pale sunlight filtered through, a blue snake lay coiled. I picked up a stone.

"Don't throw it," spoke Sàndor, touching my arm. He crawled up through the rocks behind and made a dive for the tail as it slid out of sight.

"Ah! Just missed it."

"Was it poisonous?"

"No. Usually they're easy to catch."

"What do you do with them?"

"Let them go, keep them as pets. Sometimes I let one loose in Giovanni's house."

I went cautiously by where the snake had been. We climbed and swam, saw fish in the clear pools. In a sandy place I found tracks and pointed them out to Sàndor.

"Ronsocco."

"What's that?"

"River pig. We hunt them at night."

At last we became tired and turned back, allowing the waterfalls to wash us down into the pools, then swimming to the next waterfall. We found our clothes and spread them out to dry on the limbs of a dead tree near the deserted lumber camp.

"How far are we from your house now?"

"About two miles. If you walk to the top of the ravine and climb a tree, you can see it clearly."

"It's cool here. I thought the jungle would be hotter."

"This is high jungle—two thousand feet."

"Now that the house is completed I suppose you'll begin to develop the farm."

"I don't care about the farm."

"What about the seedlings?"

"No cleared land to plant them on."

"Your men have begun to cut down the trees."

"Five or six more years to wait after that."

"At least you've got the house."

"If I didn't have that house I wouldn't be in Tingo Maria. I want to live here and get down to Lima when I feel like it. That's all."

"What about money?"

"The bank lends me money for the farm."

"What do you do with it?"

"Take a trip to Lima, buy more bricks or a refrigerator."

"They must check up on you."

"Occasionally Cruz comes around. I show him the seedlings, tell him I am disgusted that Tingo Maria is no good for coffee."

"Just a good place to live."

"I say I'm so disgusted with the poor quality of the land, so poor that even the seedlings won't grow without layers of expensive fertilizer, that I am thinking seriously about leaving."

"Then what happens?"

"The bank gives me more money."

"Why?"

"They think: one day that son of a bitch Sàndor will become bored sitting alone in his brick house doing nothing. He'll go out and begin clearing the land and plant the seedlings. Then we'll get our money back."

"Perhaps they're right."

"Never. Already there's such a surplus of coffee in the world that in Brazil half the crop is burned or thrown into the sea, just to get rid of it."

"Is that why you refuse to produce any more?"

"Growing coffee doesn't interest me at all."

"How long can this last?"

"I don't know. So far I've had the opportunity to build the house and do what I want."

"Tingo Maria must be a good place to live."

"We have very good air here."

We lay in the sun and dozed until the clothes dried. Sàndor got to his feet and stretched. He seemed to belong to the jungle.

I stayed with Sàndor for a week. Each day we walked into the forest and swam in the river. Sometimes we went into town to see what was going on. Nothing ever was. Living in that house with only Vasil around must have been lonesome for Sàndor, although he never admitted it. In the afternoons we always paid Giovanni a visit. The three of us swam and played checkers on a stump near the river bank until the sun went down. Giovanni's house is located on a low bluff overlooking the river. Above it, in the branches of trees and stretched between long poles stuck into the ground, was a complicated network of wires and antennae. Giovanni is a ham radio operator and communicates with people all over the world. He had been living in Tingo Maria nine years and although he had developed a productive coffee plantation since then, he remained as much in debt to the bank as Sàndor. This fact didn't seem to worry him.

We ate dinner in a large open-air room, just a platform with a thatch roof and fine protective screening all around. Afterwards Giovanni turned on the radio. Sàndor and I sat down to play more checkers; Elizabeth, Giovanni's wife, read and looked on.

"CQ, CQ. CQ Stateside. CQ 20 Stateside. This is OA3I Ocean Able Three Item, calling anyone Stateside. CQ 20 America."

"Sàndor, how old are you?"

"Twenty-nine."

"CQ, CQ. CQ 20 Stateside. OA3I in Tingo Maria, Peru."

"Why do you ask?"

"Quiet, Sàndor! I'm trying to make contact with someone in America!"

"You play checkers very well."

"CQ Stateside. CQ 20 Stateside. This is Ocean Able Three Item in Tingo Maria, Peru. What say, Stateside?"

"Elizabeth, who's that Indian girl I see around here, about fifteen years old?"

"Juana. She takes care of the children."

"While I was in the bedroom putting on my bathing suit, she was looking in through the window."

"Yes?"

"CQ, CQ."

"What did you do to her?"

"Later I went around the corner of the house to change back into my clothes. There she was looking out through the window."

"CQ Stateside."

"What did you do?"

"Shut up, Sàndor! CQ Stateside. CQ 20 Stateside."

"Just went on changing. It's hard to see someone through that fine screening. But she's always there."

"She's ready, that girl."

"You leave her alone, Sàndor," said Elizabeth.

Large insects clung to the wire mesh, trying to get in at the light.

"All right, read you loud and clear, WC2JH. You're putting in a strong signal tonight. Copy you one hundred per cent. This is OA3I, Ocean Able Three Item. QTH is Tingo Maria, Peru. Johnny's the handle. Give me your QTH again. Go ahead, old man."

Sàndor was concentrating on his checkers.

"Elizabeth, does this go on every night?"

"Every night is the same."

"Albany, New York. Well, Sam, this is Johnny speaking. I'm out here in the jungle, Sam, Peruvian rain forest on the eastern side of the Andes Mountains. Let me give you that QTH again, Sam. That's Texas Italia Napoli Genova Ohio Milano Argentina Roma Italia Argentina. Go ahead."

From the darkness outside the rush of the river was audible.

"Sam, get a map and look for the Huallaga River, about three hundred miles northeast of Lima. I'm a farmer, Sam, have a coffee farm right on the banks of the Huallaga River. Could throw a rock into it from where I'm sitting."

"Whom does he talk to?"

"Anybody he can contact, but mostly America and Italy."

"All right, Sam, you're still putting in a fine signal. Here it is again: Honolulu Uruguay Argentina London London Argentina Guatamala Argentina. That's a river. Go ahead, Sam."

"Where did he get this set?"

"Same place where my bricks come from."

"The bank, what do they say about it?"

"That's right, Sam, we're in the Peruvian jungle. Very tropical here, big trees, animals running around—snakes, lions, tigers, that sort of thing, elephants. . . ."

"Giovanni!"

"Plenty hot here. How's the weather up in Albany, New York, Sam? Back to you."

"He tells Cruz he uses it to keep in touch with the coffee prices in Lima. When the prices are up, he ships the coffee; when they are low he hangs onto the coffee, and waits."

"Does Cruz believe him?"

"I don't think so."

"Cold. Well, Sam, it's plenty hot here, I tell you that. Sam, I've got a couple of your countrymen right here beside me in the shack. Matter of fact, I'm married to an American. Wife's an American, Sam. Back to you."

Sàndor takes his checkers very seriously and beat me in a careful match.

"More checkers, Caffery?"

"You're beginning to fade, Sam, you're fading. Can you read me? WC2JH, Albany, New York, this is OA3I. Do you still copy? Go ahead."

"Sàndor, you must play checkers every night."

"What else is there to do?"

"Sam, you're still fading. Some QSB on this frequency now and I'm having trouble reading you. Sam, I'm on this frequency every night at the same time, always looking for someone to talk to, anybody who will answer my signal. WC2JH, WC2JH,

Albany, New York, this is OA3I, Ocean Able Three Item. Do you still copy? Seventy-three and standing by for any possible final."

■ ■ ■

One morning Sàndor announced that he must drive to town for supplies. I said I'd pack my bag and go with him.

"No! You can't leave so soon!"

"I've stayed too long already."

"I told Giovanni you'd be here for a month. When the moon comes out we're going to shoot *ronsoccos* in the forest."

"I ought to be on my way."

"We'll take a canoe trip up the river, go fishing and hunting."

"Sàndor, I can't."

"Caffery, please stay."

"No, Sàndor, I better go into town with you."

We drove into Tingo Maria with Vasil riding behind in an open trailer. I got off at the hotel.

"Caffery, we can hunt *ronsoccos* tonight in the dark if you stay."

Vasil climbed down from the trailer and took my place in the Land Rover. His dark suit and bushy eyebrows were white with dust.

"Sàndor, are you going to live in Tingo Maria forever?"

"I don't plan to be in any place forever. But you come back with me and sleep one more night in the house, Caffery."

"If the bank takes away the house, what will you do?"

"I don't know. I'll go to Cruz right now and get money to buy bullets. I'll tell him *ronsoccos* are eating my seedlings."

"Where will you go?"

"I don't know. *Ronsoccos* are good to eat."

"Lima?"

"Perhaps. I can live anywhere."

"I'm going down the river."

"Caffery, stay in Tingo Maria for a while. Maybe we can do something together, like revamp the lumberyard. All that machinery belongs to the bank. Cruz will be glad to get rid of it and I can talk him into financing a new operation."

"It's already failed once."

"There's plenty of wood in the forest. We'll try again."

"I don't know, Sàndor. My plans are indefinite. I might keep on going and exit through the rivers, I might come back."

"Come back to Tingo Maria. We'll strip naked and hunt those *ronsoccos* in the river with knives between our teeth like the Indians."

"Is that the way they hunt them, with knives?"

"That's what Giovanni says. Get back in this car and we'll go after them tonight."

"No, Sàndor, I'll stay here."

"Hasta luego, then."

"Hasta luego."

He drove off.

At dinner all the Indian waiters crowded around my table so they would have something to do. Except for me the place was empty. It was a well-constructed hotel, built of polished natural hardwood from the forest, and they were proud of it. I had a private cabin near the river and slept well. It rained heavily all night. The constant drumming on the tin roof has a soporific effect, and if I ever woke up the sound of that rain put me back to sleep again. By this time I was being badly bitten by mosquitoes. There seem to be two species here: one goes for your ankles, wrists, and knuckles and leaves tiny blood blisters called *sangrecitos.* The other attacks the back and belly, where red welts rise. Both itch horribly.

The next day I was in town wondering how I was going to get out of it. The airport was flooded; the road to Pucallpa had been cut. Walking along the river where women pounded their clothes with stones, I came across two Indians completing the construction of a balsa raft. I sat down on a rock and watched them for a while. I like to see men work with their hands.

"Where are you going?"

They looked at me and went back to work chopping and shaping the balsa logs.

"Bella Vista."

The two were working waist deep in the water. The younger one was heavily built, the older, the one who spoke, lean.

"When do you leave?"

The logs were joined to the crosspieces by bark straps. All work was done with machetes.

"Mañana."

The Huallaga is about eighty yards across and running deep. On the far side black vultures hunch on boulders. Garbage from the town is dumped there. I hadn't seen any of those birds up in the Sierra. Too high for them up there.

"Take a passenger?"

"Sí."

"How many days is the trip?"

"Cinco, cuatro dias."

We made a price of fifty *soles* for the trip. I ran off into town and bought a machete and enough food for a week. The rest of the day I spent trying to sharpen the machete on a rock.

That evening I told the waiters at the hotel that I would be leaving in the morning.

"Señor," one replied sadly, *"usted nos dejará vacío.* You will leave us empty."

The others nodded their heads as they stood silently around my table, their hands clasped behind their backs.

■　■　■

The next morning early I walked into town on a muddy road, avoiding the puddles. Clouds clung to the dark forested hills across the river. It looked to me as if it were never going to stop raining.

Nobody was on the raft. Since yesterday a raised platform had been built above the base logs, covering the forward half of the raft. I threw my gear down on this and waited for the raftmen to return. Reflecting the dark saturated sky, the water looked black. Above the rush of the river I could hear the women pounding their clothes near the bridge. Soon the raftmen approached, carrying large cardboard cartons, which they set down heavily on the platform.

"What's that?"

"Beer."

"Who's going to drink it?"

"The people in Bella Vista."

They made several trips until the raft was loaded. The one called Ossorio went off again while the other placed banana leaves over the boxes. His name was Juan. Then while I watched, he bound two large wooden blades to long poles. These were to be the sweeps. With his machete he sharpened some lengths of hard wood. Then he picked up a stone off the bank and hammered the sharpened ends right into the outside balsa logs of the raft. As he worked all the muscles of his body were visible. The sticks were angled so four of them came together and could be secured near the top like a tepee. The sweeps pivoted in the V thus formed.

"Juan, how often do you make this trip?"

"Every three or two weeks."

"Do you always carry beer?"

"We carry anything, even passengers."

Juan explained that they built the raft in Tingo Maria, loaded it with beer or whatever they were commissioned to carry, and floated down to Bella Vista, where they unloaded the cargo and sold the raft. Then they returned by plane with only the sweep blades, which had been carved from a particularly hard wood and required much work to replace. It looked like mahogany to me.

Ossorio returned with an armful of salted fish and a package of rice. The cargo was tied down with the same bark strips— they are soaked in water and shrink to tremendous tension —and we shoved off. It took the three of us to lever the raft off the rocks. Juan and Ossorio handled the long sweeps until the current caught us, then rested, and in motionless river silence we were swept down under the green suspension bridge with a broken cable trailing in the water, past the tin and board shacks of Tingo Maria under the pall of cook smoke, past the buzzards hunched on river boulders, and around a bend between solid green forest walls.

All that morning we passed huts along the shore and canoes tied to the overhanging trees or being paddled upstream in the easy water near the bank. Occasionally I saw smoke rising from a clearing in the forest. The sound of an axe came to us across the water. Towards noon we passed a long dugout canoe coming noisily upriver. Three Indians crouched together in the bow with the gear piled up in the middle. A heavy-set white man in a wide straw hat was seated in the stern operating the outboard motor. The Indians waved but the big man in the back just glanced at me and kept his eyes fixed upriver. He might be Belgian, I thought, for the whole lot looked straight out of the Belgian Congo.

Most of the day I sat up on the beer, smoking and watching, feeling an adventurous solitude. Juan and Ossorio pulled on the sweeps to keep the raft in the channel and waited, with the dripping mahogany blades suspended above the swirling surface. When the sun came out hot, we all plunged into the muddy water for a swim. Actually we didn't do much swimming, but just hung onto the raft as it spun downstream. It's a good feeling to lie there in the water and watch the forest slide by, and to have the whole river slide along with you.

At five o'clock we tied up before a cluster of stick huts atop caving mud banks. This was a town called Pucante. Juan and Ossorio went off while I stayed with the raft and watched a group of naked Indian children with distended bellies splash around in the shallows. The people who live along this river look yellow to me. The children went away after a while and I stretched out on the beer boxes to take a siesta.

Juan and Ossorio returned before dark. I didn't know where they had been, but they travel this river frequently and must have friends in these towns. Juan cooked dinner over three stones on the river bank. I insisted we eat my food and we ate nearly all of it. Afterwards we smoked cigarettes and drank pisco out of a tin cup. It was good being with these two.

When the fire died down there was nothing to do but try and get some sleep. Juan and Ossorio spread palm fronds in the bottom of a rotten dugout canoe half buried in the mud and went right to sleep. Meanwhile I groped about in the dark looking for some comfortable place. Finally I crawled back on the raft. Lightning was flickering far away. I lay down and listened to the sound of the river. The mosquitoes were a nuisance.

Gradually the wind began to rise and the lightning illuminated whitecaps across the dark moving expanse of water. The rivermen stirred and Ossorio came over and touched my shoulder.

"Amigo, venga. Va a llover mucho."

I followed them into a small deserted hut, where Juan indicated that I sleep on a raised platform in the corner. They spread a grass mat on the floor and went back to sleep. As I lay down the rain began to fall, and the thatch roof didn't catch all of it. Nevertheless, this platform was more comfortable than the raft. I was moving towards sleep when something ran across me. I turned the flashlight on a brown rat perched on my boot, its eyes glistening in the light. Now I had the loaded pistol by my side and my first impulse was to shoot it. However, I'm not a good shot and might easily put a bullet into my foot. Besides, the report of the gun would bring the whole village running. So I just moved my boot slightly to one side and the rat jumped away. I had a feeling he intended to eat the rawhide laces. For the rest of the night I lay there sleepless and uneasy, from time to time playing the flashlight around. All kinds of animals might seek refuge from the rain in this hut.

The next morning before dawn we pushed the raft off the mud into the opaque current of the Huallaga. I felt sick: some stomach disorder was giving me cramps and fever. I vomited into the river, swallowed some enterovioform, and lay down on the beer, watching the dark vegetal façade slip by.

"Estoy enfermo."

Juan and Ossorio looked at me unconcernedly as they worked the sweeps. The river was broader here—almost twice its width at Tingo Maria and still flowing fast. The country had flattened out. Parrots raced through the reddish sky, screaming and diving. I prefer the desert to this wilderness. At least you can see where you are and where you're going. I missed Lima and the highway heading north along the coast.

By noon I felt better, having watched Juan erect a cooking platform with four green sticks pounded upright into the balsa, attaching crosspieces to make a level platform, and covering it with earth. We pulled the salted fish apart with our fingers and ate the rice and long green bananas roasted in the coals. Drinking water remained a problem: it takes a long time to boil, squeeze in a lemon, and wait for it to cool. Finally I just got down on my hands and knees like Ossorio and drank out of the river. Later I took out a heavy handline Bonsal had given me, baited the large hook with a piece of banana, and tried my luck. Within a minute I had dragged in a sluggish fish about two feet long, with thick red and brown scales. It looked like a change of diet to me but Juan and Ossorio shook their heads. The fish was inedible. I caught several more of the same before quitting.

They snap ravenously at the banana as soon as it hits the water, but give up when hooked. My arms grew tried of towing them in.

We continued until long after dark, when the rush of the river becomes ominous. At last Ossorio tied up to a tree in some easy water below a sand bar. I followed my guides for a mile over a trail to a clearing in the jungle. Before a large cane house about thirty Indians were sitting around several fires. While they welcomed Juan and Ossorio I put my bag down among the thick roots of a tree. Some children gathered around to watch me. In the firelight their large eyes looked solidly black and sightless. One let his hand stray towards my boot and, when I made no move to interfere, ran it over the leather, entwining his fingers in the laces. I pulled out the Swiss knife, which was such a success that it drew half the men away from the fire. After food there was some storytelling. A large snake had been killed that day. The skin was displayed. Not much remained, so many machetes had hacked at it. In the dark I couldn't tell its size, but it was long enough that one man was unable to hold it off the ground. The eyes and teeth of the Indians glittered in the flickering light. At length the fires died down and we all lay together on the mat floor of the house. With so many sleeping bodies around me the jungle noises grew remote. I managed to get some sleep.

The following day the character of the river changed as it surged through a range of low hills. Juan was jumping back and forth between his sweep and the beer cases. I never saw a man so alert as when he stood on his toes and scanned downriver. We had some white water but nothing serious. When he finally saw what he was looking for he turned to me and made a circular motion with his hand.

"Remolino."

The river flowed right up against a high rock cliff with such force that a brown hill of water was formed. The circular current set up as the river backed off to the right and changed course had become an enormous whirlpool. No bottomless sucking hole existed in the center, but just below the surface there were rocks that can split a raft in two. It was impossible to avoid this vortex. As parrots wheeled and screamed over our heads, the screams echoing off the white cliffs, Juan and Ossorio laboured to keep the raft from being drawn down into the cavity of water. All I could do was sit on the beer and anxiously wait.

The raft broke free at last but was swept immediately into some heavy rapids. Juan and Ossorio attempted to rest on the sweeps for a moment and seemed to lose control. The raft went sideways over a submerged boulder and began to cant over so much that I thought the beer and everything else would shift into the river. One whole side was lifted out of the water and would not recover until the three of us scrambled to the upper edge and managed to weigh it down. Meanwhile one of the sweeps was loose in the white water. Ossorio dove for it and clambered back onto the raft, the water streaming off his body. I like these days when one's actions take on importance.

The Huallaga seemed bigger and faster every mile now. At bends where the channel is forced to the outside, whole sections of the bank are ripped away. Great trees fall booming into the flood with vines and branches snapping and jerking. They slowly get under way as the current grips them, a muddy dye spreading from the roots. Masses of this driftwood come curling downstream, some with small animals clinging to the upper branches. The trees hang up in shallow places and accumulate at the head of every island and sandspit. Green parrots roost among the bleached-out branches and roots. This debris of the forest is a hazard. Often sunken logs raked heavily across the bottom of the balsa.

I passed the time sleeping and watching the jungle slide by. Once I saw a bright green snake winding among the smooth stones of a sand bar. As usual, my first impulse was to have a shot at it, but my attention was caught by a movement on the opposite bank. I put the gun down. The treetops were shaking with the passage of small amber monkeys, a whole herd swinging and running along the branches, leaping right out of the foliage and falling back, hundreds of them. The colours of the trees seem a paler green here. Liana streamers hang down and stroke the water. The monkeys and snake disappeared, which was just as well: the thing about carrying a gun is that you always want to use it.

Tocache was the first good-sized town we came to. It is located atop a high mud bluff on the western bank. We tied up at the base of this bluff, a narrow shore cluttered with wrecked balsas, dugout canoes, and fishermen's shacks. The men sitting on logs before cook fires had small mongolian bodies. I noticed that several lacked fingers and even hands, and pointed this out to Ossorio.

"Piranha," he said.

When they heard this word the yellow men grinned and held up their stumps.

While Juan and Ossorio added an extra log to the raft, I put on a clean shirt and climbed the bluff, hoping to find something to eat. The town consisted of one-storey wood and corrugated metal houses set around two sides of an open area where half-naked boys shout and kick a ball. This plaza looks as if it had been planned for military parades and speeches. A few broken street lamps bend over the high grass along the edge. On the far side limbs of large trees are studded with stooped vulture forms.

My appearance attracted a gang of children who followed me to a store, where they hung around the open door and windows. The man behind the counter looked like other Greeks or Jews who have set themselves up as shopkeepers along these rivers. I asked him if he had any fresh meat for sale. He turned and shouted through the door behind him that opened onto a muddy courtyard. A boy about fourteen who looked just like him appeared with a lump of meat in his hand. The meat was old.

"What kind of meat is that?"

"Vaca."

"Are there cows in Tocache? That doesn't look like cow to me."

"Sí, señor, es carne de vaca."

"Is that all you have?"

"Tengo chancho. Quiere comprar un chancho?" . .

"I can't eat a whole pig. What else do you have? Chicken?"

The boy was still holding the meat out in both hands like an offering. The man shook his head. *"No hay pollo."*

"Nothing but this meat here? Tell him to take it away. I don't want it. What else do people eat in this town?"

The man cracked his knuckles. *"Paujíles."*

"Turkeys? I'll take one. Where are they?"

"En la selva."

"Wild turkey. *Hay mucho?*"

"Sí mucho."

"Easy to shoot?"

"Sí."

"Do you have a gun?"

"Quiere comprar un fusil?"

"No, I want to shoot a turkey. I'll rent the gun from you and buy the shells."

The boy was still standing there holding out the meat. The man sent him after the gun.

A few minutes later I stepped out into the sun with an old single-shot gun and five shells in my pocket. The boy came along as guide. We walked back through the muddy streets of the town and out across a swampy savannah. The wingless fusilage of an old plane lay half sunken in the water with a clump of tall grass growing around. I think there used to be an airport out here. We crossed the swamp and came among a wreckage of fallen trees. The boy pointed to a large black vulture perched in the upper branches of a dead tree, the rotting branches white against the forest.

"Paujíl!"

"That's no turkey, boy, that's a vulture."

I took a shot at it anyway and missed. The report died over the swamp as the bird flapped heavily away.

"Is that what you call a turkey in this town?"

I broke the rusty gun over my knee and inserted another shell.

"I don't have to leave the pensión to shoot one of those birds—just open the window and fire as they float by."

We wandered through the half cleared and rotting forest, the spectral trees reflected in pools of water. Some of these trees grow so thickly together that even dead ones do not fall, but remain locked in the grip of others. Wild orchids cling to the decomposing trunks. It looked like a place for birds and crocodiles, but nothing moved. I expended the rest of my shells on a bunch of wild bananas and walked back to town.

The bluff was casting its shadow across the river towards the blackening shapes of the hills to the east. One after another the vultures left their roosts at the edge of the jungle and flew in low over the town with a dry rush of wings. From the riverbank below rose the smell of fish being fried in oil, of bananas being roasted. Women carefully descend to collect water in buckets and cans. The children follow, sliding down the hill in the mud. Out on the river men called to one another. A machete was being sharpened on a rock. Someone laughed, and darkness fell.

Juan and Ossorio went off into town after dinner. I prepared myself a bed of palm fronds on the mud bank and lay there sleepless as usual, listening to the sound of the river and waiting for them to return. These river nights are extremely warm and comfortable, but I find it difficult to enjoy them. I never feel at ease in the jungle, never prepared. It's impossible to shake off that slight, constant fear of surprise.

They came back after midnight very drunk but careful not to disturb me as they lay down on either side of me. I think they know I sleep better when they are around.

It was still dark when I snapped awake. Something out in the river was howling and snuffling. I looked at my watch—exactly four o'clock—and remembered Paul's words about snakes coming out only at night to hunt along the riverbank. The noise sounded like a cow caught in a trap, heavy whistling and breathing, or being smothered to death. I felt for my pistol and played the flashlight around the area, but saw nothing but the shapes of canoes and balsa logs. The moaning ceased so only the rush of the river was audible. I had to get off this bank now. I set my watch ahead an hour and shook Juan.

"Juan, Ossorio, vamos. Son las cinco. Vamos!"

They were still drunk and incredulous that it could be five o'clock already, but got up and stumbled onto the raft. The howling commenced once more, a low strangling noise.

"Listen! What is that?"

They sprawled out on the beer cases and fell asleep immediately. I pushed off and handled the sweeps until we were in midriver. The noise subsided into a long groan as we floated away on the black water, the rising vapor visible in the first light.

The sun rose over a river broader than ever. All morning I lay in my place on the beer while the two rivermen took turns sleeping and working the sweeps. It was hot and we swam several times. Once I floated beside the raft for so long that I nearly fell asleep in the warm swirling water.

From a breadth of more than two hundred yards the river narrowed throughout the day until it was rushing down a slot between chalk cliffs less than thirty yards apart. Vines and streamers hung down and jerked in the current, snapping across the raft. Red and yellow parrots with long blue tail feathers dove down from their nests on the cliffs, screaming above the roar of the river. We were approaching some dangerous rapids. While Ossorio checked the lashings of the logs and cargo, even strapping me down, Juan was up on the beer, peering ahead down the canyon. There was no white water yet, just deep undulating current, fast and black in the shadows of the cliffs. Suddenly he leapt down.

"Mal paso."

The sweeps were stowed and they got down. As soon as I saw it we were in it: a sliding drop and six-foot standing waves that the heavy raft plowed through, submerging us completely. I struggled against the straps, gasped for air as we came out, the spray flying, and was drowned again. The force of the water was so great that I thought the raft might break up. In another minute we were out and floating free, the water streaming off us. Juan untied me.

"That wasn't bad."

"Now, no. But in winter, when there is no rain, it is much more dangerous."

"Yes?"

"The river is lower. There are many rocks in the water. *Muy peligroso.* I've lost two rafts there."

"Yes? The beer too?"

"Claro. The beer and everything. All lost."

"And what happened to you?"

"Nothing."

I got out the pistol and cleaned it.

At dusk swarms of mosquitoes stack up in columns along the riverbank. We cooked the last of the rice and long green bananas and kept on through the night. I lay on the beer cases listening to the rush and suck of the river. The coals of the cook fire glowed in the darkness, trailing smoke and sparks over the water. Juan and Ossorio stayed on the sweeps while I slept.

Towards midnight we passed Juanjui, a big town whose lights

illuminated the river. There was music playing, and silhouettes of canoes floated near the shore. Later I was awakened by an uproar in the jungle. The channel was hugging the outside bank around a bend so we were just a few feet from the shore. Half-fallen trees thrashed in the current.

"Chancho."

Wild pig. Judging by the snorting and trampling through the undergrowth it must have been enormous, or there may have been a whole herd of them. The sound followed us along the bank until the river straightened out and the channel diverted to the middle once more.

At dawn the raft bumped against a low mud flat strewn with broken balsas and the dead wreckage of the forest. On the far side was a town, Bella Vista.

■ ■ ■

I put my gear together, paid the rivermen, and trudged off over the flats. As I entered the town my only thought was of how I was going to get out of it. Intrepid vultures perch a few feet above your head on the protruding beams of unpainted mud houses. The mud is so deep in the streets that plank bridges have been thrown across. It looks as if the Huallaga rises over its banks and flows through Bella Vista part of the year. The stagnant pools of water had not yet dried up. Everything was dead and silent at this hour, and it didn't look as if things would improve much when the people woke up. At least they have an airport in this town.

I sat down on a piece of driftwood in the main square, where the shiny mud had cracked and curled. By seven o'clock it had become so hot that I had to seek shade somewhere, and hung around the Faucett Airlines ticket office until it opened. The agent, unshaven in dirty pajamas, informed me that a plane was due in at eleven o'clock. I attempted to buy a ticket on the spot but had no Peruvian currency. I had spent most of it in Tocache and given the rest to the rivermen. The agent rubbed the sleep out of his eyes with his dirty fingers and stubbornly refused to accept a traveller's check. He said he didn't know who I was. As I pleaded he turned away and disappeared through a low opening in the mud wall.

The ticket to Yurimaguas cost only five dollars, so I tried to peddle my razor blades in the street. As I stood there in the shade watching a man wrestle with his donkey mired up to its haunches in the mud, a little barefoot boy came up and touched my hand.

"What do you want, boy?"

"Venga conmigo, señor."

"Where?"

"Venga a la Señora Gringa."

I followed him through the back streets to a whitewashed two-storey house. A large white woman opened the door, looked me up and down, and asked my name in English. I told her and she invited me in.

"What brings you to Bella Vista, Mr. Caffery?"

I replied that I had arrived this morning on a raft and was just passing through.

"I see. Will you eat some breakfast?"

"Yes, ma'am, I will."

We entered a small patio which served as a classroom. There were desks and stacks of Bibles everywhere. The teacher's table was set for one.

"Sit down there. Would you like an egg, Mr. Caffery?"

"Yes, I would."

"Like some ground peanuts?"

"Yes."

She shouted something to a servant and pulled up a chair.

"Now, how long do you plan to stay in Bella Vista?"

"I hope to leave on this morning's plane for Yurimaguas."

"So soon? That's a pity. Protestant or Catholic?"

"Protestant."

"Good. That's good, although it really doesn't matter. We had a Catholic passing through here a year ago, a young man like yourself. A nice man. American?"

"Yes."

"Good. Here's your breakfast."

A plate with one fried egg and ground peanuts was placed in front of me. As I was about to eat I saw her across the desk, with her red hands folded and her eyes lowered.

"Please, Mr. Caffery, I saw that you were hungry the moment I opened the door, but can't you wait while I thank the Lord for this food?"

I put my fork down and waited.

"Now, Mr. Caffery, some coffee?"

"Yes, ma'am."

"You haven't asked my name, Mr. Caffery."

I put my fork down again.

"Mrs. Hornby. That's my maiden name, although I'm married. You didn't think Señora Gringa was my real name, did you?"

"No, I didn't."

"Are you married, Mr. Caffery?"

"No."

I mixed the peanuts and the egg yolk together. "Have you been in Bella Vista for some time, Mrs. Hornby?"

"I came here thirty-four years ago, up the river in a canoe from Iquitos."

"You've been in this town thirty-four years?"

"I was only eighteen years old and have not left since."

"Thirty-four years without ever leaving?"

"Does that seem like a long time to you, Mr. Caffery?"

"Yes, it does."

"Thirty-four years and every moment harassed by those awful bigoted priests."

"What?"

"Priests they call themselves, celibates, sleeping with every innocent Indian girl on this side of the river."

I poured myself another cup of coffee.

"Have you seen those little children in the streets of this town, Mr. Caffery, the blue-eyed ones?"

"No, I don't believe I have. I just arrived this morning."

"I know perfectly well where they come from. Oh, I've had to fight them every inch of the way, but I'm not dissatisfied. Twenty-three converts, Church of England. Thirty-four years, Mr. Caffery, but I haven't been unhappy here."

"Mrs. Hornby, that's a long time to be in this town."

"Except with my husband. The day we married he ran off with all my medicines. He loaded them on a raft while I watched—I was helpless—and floated down to Iquitos, where he sold them and returned here to live on my money. He lives right upstairs with his women!" She brought her red hand down on the table. "But what can I do? There is no police, no law in Bella Vista."

"I didn't think so."

"It's been the only dark cloud on my life. I thought he just wanted a white woman, like so many of them do, and I was reluctant to let him touch me, fond of him as I was. At last I gave in, only to find he wanted a white woman's money."

While she talked I had been looking at my watch. It was already ten o'clock, and somehow I had to be on that plane in an hour. There was nothing to do but to explain my predicament to her. She listened, looking at me sternly.

"You are an honest man, are you not, Mr. Caffery?"

"Yes, ma'am."

"Perhaps you ought to try once more selling your razor blades."

"The Indians don't shave."

"I'm not surprised; my husband had no more than a dozen hairs on his chin and those he plucked."

"Besides, they're too poor."

"If I give you the money, you promise you will return it from Yurimaguas?"

"I'll go directly from the airport to the bank."

"One hundred and twenty *soles* is the fare, I believe."

"Yes, ma'am."

I took the money and ran to buy a ticket. As I left the office I saw Juan and Ossorio up the street. They returned my wave, but it was as if I had never been on that raft with them. Mrs. Hornby was waiting for me when I returned. I thanked her and picked up my bag.

"You're welcome, Mr. Caffery. You must be careful sending money through the post. I advise you to sew it to a piece of carbon paper before placing it in the envelope. That way no one can tell what the letter contains. Can you sew, Mr. Caffery?"

"A little."

"Although you haven't been in Bella Vista a long time, I've enjoyed your company. I don't suppose you will ever return to Bella Vista again, as you chose to remain only a few hours this time and seem so anxious to be on your way."

"I never stay long in any place."

"That may be a mistake. But I shall think of you from time to time, Mr. Caffery, and pray that you have a safe journey."

I picked up my machete which had fallen to the floor.

"Mr. Caffery, I must confess something before you go. The thought crossed my mind not to lend you that money in order to keep you here in Bella Vista with me, if only for another day. You see, I'm just an old woman, Mr. Caffery, doing God's work, but just a lonely old woman."

I carried my bag up a steep hill to a high plateau above the town where the grass airstrip is located. It must be from here that the town receives its name. I was able to see for miles. The Huallaga comes looping down through the flat rain forest, almost doubling back on itself, like a tidal creek. To keep out of the sun I sat down against the wall of the radio shack and fell asleep. When the plane came in the vultures rose from the trees and sailed out over the town.

■ ■ ■

As soon as the plane landed in Yurimaguas I went to the bank and cashed a check. I felt better with some money in my pocket. From the bank I went to the Post Office, where I mailed the price of the ticket back to Sra. Gringa in Bella Vista. After that I found a cheap hotel. The place was run by an American woman who had been living in Yurimaguas for more than fifty years, having been married to a rich Peruvian who had died long ago. Bonsal had told me about her. She gave me a room on a balcony overlooking a cobblestone courtyard. There are a lot of old women living along this river.

After a long siesta I took a walk around town. The main plaza of Yurimaguas is paved. On the corners stand large townhouses, relics from the rubber-boom days. Most of them have been abandoned or converted into brothels. The pale orange façades are latticed with moss and creepers; grass grows up in the gutters and between tiles. The iron lace balconies do not look safe. In the early evening thousands of people stroll back and forth beneath the palms and the old street lamps. From loudspeakers attached to the palm trees the usual music is broadcast. Bats as big as ducks flit through the warm night air. This is the kind of town I like.

The boat for Iquitos ties up at a pier a mile outside town. The next afternoon I picked up my bag and walked out there to see if it had come in. The dirt track by the river led among squatters' shacks and toppling reed fences. Yellow dogs snarled as I went by. Next to the dock a man was seated on the roots of a shade tree, with a line in the muddy water.

"*Hay algo de suerte?*"

"*Nada.*"

I squatted down beside him. "When does the boat arrive from Iquitos?"

"This afternoon or tomorrow."

"How long does it remain in Yurimaguas?"

"One or two days. Are you in a hurry?"

"No."

So I had plenty of time. After resting a few minutes in the shade I gave some dirty clothes to an old Indian woman to pound on the rocks and walked back toward town.

This time the dogs saw me coming. Two I hit with stones yelped and kept their distance, but a third, a mongrel with pointed ears and a long snout, kept boring in. I was forced to turn around every few steps and let fly with another rock. Finally I just stopped and put my pack down. This dog didn't look right to me. It was emaciated and the jaws were a little wet. This time I hit it squarely in the ribs, but it only snarled and kept on circling. The sun beat down hard on the dry road. Nobody was around. The dog circled closer and did not retreat even when I raised my arm as if to throw again. Keeping an eye on it, I bent down and drew the pistol out of the pack and cocked it. I knew I shouldn't do this, but to be bitten in Yurimaguas by a possibly rabid dog scared me. In vain I hurled one more stone, which missed, kicking up the dust and bounding away. Up and down the eroded track no one was in sight. When the dog bore in again I shot it.

The instant I saw the dog twisting on the ground I was sorry I'd done it. Without making a sound it was miserably attempting to drag itself away on its front feet. The bullet had passed through the hindquarters. The first report had already been too loud, but I had no choice but to step forward and shoot it through the back of the head. The jaws opened and snapped shut, the yellow canine teeth protruding. Drops of blood were sprinkled on the light dust.

Several people were immediately visible on the road. As I put the gun away a man dashed out from the shacks and confronted me. Looking from me to the dead animal he stated in a calm voice that I had killed his dog.

"It was sick. Look at it yourself. It's jaws are wet. I think it had hydrophobia."

The man went down on one knee and examined the dog. The jaws were wet, but in this river heat I suppose it's not abnormal for an animal to sweat.

"No, that's not true. This was a good dog."

"He tried to bite me."

"This dog did not bite. You must have molested it, thrown stones at it."

"That's true, but only to keep it away."

"For that reason he wanted to bite you."

He lifted up the dead dog and put it over his shoulder.

"We shall go to the police together."

"All right."

He was a reasonable man and I had no choice but to do as he said.

We walked past the impassive staring Indians right through the main streets of the town. This man Robles, short with a sparse mustache, said he used to be a raftman. "I've had this dog a long time. I used to take him with me on the long trips."

I told Robles that I had just come downriver on a raft myself, all the way from Tingo Maria. He nodded his head and said there was less traffic on the river now than in former days.

At the police station we sat on a wooden bench, the dead dog on the floor before us. There was blood on Robles' white shirt. I told him that I was sorry, but the dog had been sick and aggressive. It had made me afraid.

"You were afraid of a dog like that?"

I asked him if he knew what hydrophobia was.

"Yes, but that dog doesn't have hydrophobia."

"How can you be sure?"

"He's my dog, isn't he? He barks at strangers, but that doesn't mean he's sick. All dogs bark at strangers, particularly ones that throw stones."

"He looked sick to me."

A man in a blue suit inspected my papers. The fact that I had a permit for the pistol seemed to make a favourable impression on him. Nevertheless, he declared that I would have to stay in jail until the dog was examined.

"You put a man in jail for shooting a sick dog?"

"The dog will be examined, *señor*."

■ ■ ■

The jail is located down by the river. I was put into a small cell that contained one wooden box and a mattress in the corner. There was nothing to do but to sit down on the box and look out through the low barred window at the river. The cell seems to be directly over the water.

This is a big river here, the Huallaga. At Tarapoto it has been joined by the Rio Mayo. It looks a half mile wide at least.

Cane houses hang out over the bank, supported by struts and pilings driven into the water. Tied to the pilings are all kinds of canoes, rowboats, big rafts with thatch huts on them, sampans, and barges. Makeshift catwalks have been thrown up between them. Part of the population of Yurimaguas lives permanently on these craft.

While old men fish, children splash around in the shallows and women pound clothes with round stones. Even that old woman is down there washing my pants in the muddy water. They can't see me up here.

Every few minutes I get up and restlessly explore the cell. A trap door in the floor just lifts open, revealing the mud and water below. In the end, however, I always go back to my box next to the window.

There's something exotic about these river towns. Yurimaguas is the first one I have come to where I wouldn't mind staying for a while, or living. I wonder what I could do in a place like this.

At seven o'clock the sun set at the end of the river. After dark they led me out to a smoky hut, where the guard and I ate fried fish out of enamel bowls. When we finished he went off to buy cigarettes while I had another piece of papaya. The night air along these rivers is extremely warm and agreeable.

I woke up at midnight from a bad dream and for a moment didn't know where I was. The frogs were making a racket out in the river. I got to my feet and stumbled against the wall. It was damp now. I opened the trap door and let it fall shut. There would be no sense in escaping. But it was so black and silent in this cell. All I could hear was the sound of my own breath and the scrape of my boots on the stone, as I crawled over the floor groping for my matches. I could not find them. Sitting upright in the corner with my knees drawn in, I tried to calm myself, but the harsh breathing was still in my ears. A horrible sense of dislocation came over me.

Feeling my way along the wall, I came to the window and touched the matches and cigarettes wedged between the bars. I struck a match and looked at my hands. The match went out, but I gratefully struck another, lit a cigarette, and wiped my face with my arm. With the cigarette glowing between my fingers I took a seat on the box and looked out.

The big rafts in midstream were discernible by their still-glowing campfires. I was glad of that. That was a good trip with

Juan and Ossorio. I wish I were with them again. They must be back in Tingo Maria by now, thinking about another balsa. Juan reckoned he's made that trip more than a hundred times.

The Huallaga flows slowly. It takes a long time for the rafts to slip by. I could hear the raftmen calling to each other. On such a calm night their voices carry a long distance across the water. What they said was impossible to make out, but it didn't matter. It was just good to hear their voices. I suppose Giovanni must still be talking to his radio at this hour or playing checkers with Sàndor. Elizabeth would be looking on and the big insects would be clotting up against the wire mesh, trying to get in at the light. I'm glad I met them.

For a long time I sat there watching the fires and listening to the raftmen's fading conversations as the river carried them away. Paul told me to think about Lima while on this trip. I have and I know that it will be good to return there.

In the morning I was awakened by a lot of bells and tinklings. By this time I felt a kind of allegiance to this jail. Not much later they let me out. Robles' dog didn't have hydrophobia but was found to have been very sick. I paid him 250 *soles* out of my pocket and walked into town. A few minutes later I was in the market with a green melon under my arm, looking at all the fish they pull out of that river. When I sat down at a table in the street with a glass of black coffee and my melon before me, some spectators stood partially concealed in the shadows of the palms. Finally they moved off, and I sliced open the big melon with my knife.

The old lady met me at the door of the hotel. She was somewhat dirty and disheveled, but she had preserved her independence. For some reason she insisted upon giving me her own room this time. It contained an old bronze bed, stacks of yellow newspapers along the walls, and nothing else. Except for the musty smell of those old newspapers it was clean. The sun shining through the open French window cast the shadow of the iron lace balcony on the floor. There was a view of the river. The steamer was just visible coming upstream from Iquitos. At last the old woman shut the door behind her, and I sat down on the edge of the bed.

■ ■ ■

The captain of the ship was an old German who said he'd been navigating these rivers for forty years. He showed me a small room containing four bunks that looked as if they'd been designed for Japanese. Rather than even attempt to sleep there I walked back into town and bought myself a big red and yellow hammock at the market. This I slung amidships where a lot of other Indians had their hammocks.

A barge was being tied alongside, as three hundred recruits for the Peruvian army were on their way to be transported to Iquitos for training. There had been some recent trouble along the Ecuadorian border. Some cargo was being taken on board, including turkeys and crates of large turtles with red numbers painted on their undersides.

The recruits arrived in the late afternoon. I never saw such a lot. Most of them looked as if they'd been pulled straight out of the jungle. An hour later we cast off, the old engines pushing the boat in a wide arc while the recruits made a terrible noise waving and shouting goodbye to their mothers and cousins on the shore. No sooner did Yurimaguas disappear around the first bend than they set up a clamour for dinner, banging their tin cups and plates on the railing and harassing the cook. You couldn't even hear the old engines turning over.

Dinner consisted of beans and rice and fried yucca. I had to sit next to the captain and listen to him talk in his bad English about the forty years on the rivers. Afterwards I lay in my hammock and looked down at the recruits crowded into the barge.

They were just boys. The smaller ones huddled in the bottom, the bilge water sloshing at their feet, and stared back at me with wild black eyes.

The hammock next to mine was occupied by a boy named Pedro who spent all his time cleaning an automatic shotgun. He was going hunting in Iquitos. I showed him my pistol. The next morning early we went up on the roof to shoot crocodiles, which infest this river. We waited for an hour until the boat swung with the channel close to the shore.

Pedro touched my arm. "I think I see a crocodile!"

"Where?"

"Among the weeds there, next to that fallen tree!"

"Pedro, is that a crocodile or a log?"

"There's only one way to find out."

We blazed away at it until the captain stuck his head up and shook his fist at us. When the shooting died down the recruits could be heard yelling and screaming. They had been asleep and probably thought the war with Ecuador had started. From that moment the captain and I were no longer friends.

In the late afternoons thunderstorms used to gather down-river. The wind raised whitecaps on the water. The passengers would get under cover at the last minute as if the thing were unexpected. All kinds of things used to get blown overboard—hammocks, cane chairs, clothing that had been hung up to dry, chickens that had been wandering free on deck. Meanwhile on the open barge the recruits sat out in the downpour. The air cleared afterwards, and everyone came out to wait for the sunset.

Every evening before dusk this woodburner stopped at certain clearings along the bank where fuel had been chopped and piled. The recruits took these opportunities to charge ashore and forage on their own. Lemons and bananas were what they wanted. They went up the lemon trees like monkeys, tearing off whole branches and throwing stones and sticks at the fruit they could not reach. Of course the banana trees were just pulled to the ground and trampled in the confusion. Once a recruit climbed on the thatch roof of the woodcutter's house after a lemon that had fallen there. He disappeared through the roof, and the whole house collapsed on top of him as the woodcutter and his family stood impassively watching. While all three hundred recruits were occupied in this way, the engineer and his two assistants loaded several cords of wood. So these stops always lasted a long time. The mosquitoes become unbearable after sunset.

On the third day the Ucayali flowing from the south joined the Marañón in a long sweep of water to form the Amazon. Although the Atlantic lay three thousand miles to the east the river was already a mile wide.

It is extremely peaceful on a river of this size. There are no swirls or eddies on the surface to indicate current. The boat appears to be plowing through a dead calm, the engines barely audible. Most of the time I lay in the hammock with my legs hanging over. Time passes more slowly than on a balsa. There is no opportunity to fish or swim or cook your own meals. The heat seems more oppressive over such a broad expanse of water. The banks are just low silhouette strips on the horizon. All rapids and whirlpools have been left far behind on the Huallaga, and with them the excitement and fear for the vulnerability of the raft and ourselves upon it.

Until I made this trip Peru seemed to be made up of brown dust and the gray Pacific. The streets of Lima were often bare. Sounds such as dogs barking and various city noises stressed my own isolation against a backdrop that seemed as lonely as I. Perhaps that's why I loved it. I don't think the jungle has meant as much.

On the fourth morning we arrived in Iquitos. It is another

one of these rubber boom towns, with the usual crumbling Spanish façades, customs sheds, and half the people living on the water. I visited the snake farm and rode around town in a bus full of musicians hired to entertain the passengers. That night I spent in a wonderful brothel with white gauze mosquito netting over the beds. The next day I flew back to Lima.

···
iii

I was on my way back from walking among the dusty hills out-side Lima. A gang of ragged youths pelted me with stones in an empty lot. I ran and jumped on a passing tram full of Indians returning from a bullfight. The tram screeched around a corner, and I hung on to the rail with one hand, attempting to pay the conductor with the other amidst the press and chatter of the In-dians. I had to flatten up against the other passengers to avoid being sideswiped by a truck, and when I got down a few blocks later and made my way through the crowds along Abancay, I thought how good it was to be back in this city.

The Indians downstairs said that Anne was in her room. I went up and crossed the roof so cautiously that she didn't hear me coming. For a minute I stood in the open door and watched her sitting on the bed. At last she looked up.

"Caffery, I didn't see you there."

I entered and sat down on the wooden chair. "You're not surprised to see me?"

"No, I knew you'd be coming back."

The room was very dark. I could see only her profile before the window.

"Are you in Paul Bonsal's flat now?"

"Yes."

"How do you like it?"

Out on the street someone was blowing a trumpet.

"I like it very much. From his terrace I have a view all the way to Callao."

"You see, I told you the weather makes a big difference."

"The sky is filled with buzzards. I like to watch them."

"They roost in the old man's trees."

"The roof tops all over Lima are flat and dusty, with shacks and chicken coops built on them. You know, a large number of people in this city live on roofs."

"What else do you see?"

"Parks, churches, and parade grounds. All the big buildings —the ministries and the banks, the red brick walls and towers of the prison, the stadium, everything." I got up and walked around the room. "Down below a beggar waits at the intersection. His legs have been amputated, but he's got a trundle some-one made for him which he wheels up and down the sidewalk. When the cars stop for the red light, he asks the passengers for money. But sometimes he just sits on the grassy strip that divides the street and whistles. You should hear him—it sounds like a three-toned flute."

"You see how pleasant it is in summer, Caffery?"

"At night Plaza San Martín is full of sleeping bodies. I don't know where they come from."

"They leave the slums to sleep on the grass."

"On my way here I met a man selling tiny green parrots. I wanted to buy one for you, but I couldn't find a cage. He said they had come right out of the nest, but I'm not so sure. Some-one told me they're called *chiquititos* because they never grow. He had spider monkeys, too."

Later Anne and I went out to the restaurant near the railroad station. As we were waiting a beggar crept in and sat down at a table near the door. He gave us a desperate glance and turned his attention back to the door, muttering something over and over.

"What's he saying?"

"Está lloviendo y los canarios están muriendose."

"What?"

"It is raining and the canaries are dying."

"How is that possible?"

"He's probably a little crazy."

Just then the waiter came over and put the man out of the restaurant. I went to the door and watched him hobble off down the street. I guess I half expected to see the rain pouring down and the gutters filled with dead canaries.

Later I took Anne to that café-bodega on the other side of the Rimac. The sad mountain music was being played on the radio behind the counter.

"Caffery, did you go to Tarapoto on your trip?"

"The plane from Bella Vista to Yurimaguas stopped there for a few minutes. I've never seen such a dusty airport."

"I know an English woman who lives in Tarapoto. Her name is Anita Juarez. While you were away she came to Lima. I saw a great deal of her and we had many long talks about her life and about mine. She said she decided a long time ago you can't live in this country without owning some land."

"She's probably right."

"She has a cattle farm in Tarapoto which she runs all by herself. It's down by the river. She invited me to come and live with her."

"Are you going?"

"I was waiting for you to return so I could tell you. I wanted to know what you thought of the idea."

"How long would you stay?"

"As long as I want. You see, I can live there for nothing."

"You won't need San Marcos any more."

"I'm tired of teaching, and besides, Caffery, I don't feel anything's happening to me here, or ever will happen. Why should these people learn English anyhow?"

"I don't know."

"I can't stand leaving Jason alone all day. I think it will be good for him to get out in the country."

"The jungle is not exactly country."

"At least it's green and open. He can grow up more or less free out there and hear something besides horns and the shouts of people selling things."

"The insects, the river at night."

"I like the jungle. I like the colours, even the insects."

"I hear they're putting a road through to Tarapoto."

"Anita told me that Tarapoto is like a frontier town. There's a sense of excitement in the air, of land being opened up. Perhaps we'll go into town on Saturday nights and have a drink at a saloon."

"They need cattle up in that part of the country. There's a shortage of meat."

"Caffery, what do you think of all this?"

"I think you ought to go."

On the way back to the tower we stopped for a moment at Plaza San Martín. High up on one of the buildings the neon dice of an advertisement rattled down over the vagrant forms stretched out on the grass.

"When will you leave for Tarapoto?"

"Soon. I've only waited for you to come back to Lima."

On Colmena we passed a construction site shielded from the street by a façade of yellow wooden bricks.

"Caffery, what are you going to do now?"

"I don't know—live here for a while and see what happens. You know I quit my job before leaving for the jungle."

"Yes, but you pay no rent."

"That's true."

"You're very fortunate, aren't you?"

"I think so."

"You're able to do exactly what you want."

Walking back to the apartment late that night, I leaned against the red wall of the prison and lit up a cigarette. I was glad that Anne was going to Tarapoto. The jungle would be good for her.

■ ■ ■

With the exception of Sra. Davis every Friday, for a month after Anne's departure I didn't see anyone. The weather was fine, and I bought myself a bamboo pole and did some fishing off the rocks. I never had any luck, and generally ended up swimming or walking from beach to beach with the pole over my shoulder. Large numbers of pelicans live along the coast.

Then one evening on the way to the cinema I met Harry in the street. He walked along beside me.

"Where have you been? Why don't I see you any more?"

"I've been travelling, Harry."

"Where?"

"Yurimaguas, Iquitos."

"It's no good there, too hot."

"I like those river towns."

"Lima is better."

"Yes. I have a new address now, Harry. It's farther away. That's why you don't see me."

I left him at Plaza San Martín and crossed the street to the theatre. When I reached into my hip pocket my wallet wasn't there. I had just cashed a check that day and all the money had been in the wallet, enough to allow me to live for a month if I was careful. Groping wildly through my jacket pockets, I looked at Harry across the street. He was standing there with his hands in his pockets and grinning at me. As we walked along together he might have put his hand on my shoulder or bumped up against me in the crowd. I can't remember.

I dodged through the heavy traffic.

"Harry, I've lost my wallet."

The grin faded. "I don't have your wallet. What do you think?"

"It was in my pocket and now it's gone."

"Here, do you want to search me?" He held his hands out from his sides.

"No, I don't want to search you, Harry."

For an instant I looked into the Indian face before dashing off through the crowd. It's at least a mile back to Bonsal's apartment and I didn't stop once. When I stumbled breathlessly up the last flight of stairs, pushed in the key, and opened the door, the wallet was lying there on the desk top. I snatched it up, saw the money was inside, and went out onto the terrace. Down the street the big Coca-Cola sign was going through its routine, throwing red reflections on the windows.

Harry was still in front of the theatre when I returned. I showed him the wallet. We sat down at a café under the arcades and talked about his passport. The grassy parts of the Plaza were beginning to fill up with sleeping forms.

"Why do they sleep out there, Harry?"

"They like to watch the lights. Lights give good dreams."

"What do you do in winter?"

"On the other side of the river a woman has two rooms. In winter she gives me one room."

"Is there a bed?"

"No, only the floor. Grass is better than a floor."

When we finished the coffee Harry got up. "I have to go to Callao now. Come with me."

"All right."

We took the tram, got down at the entrance to the port area, and walked out onto the docks. A German freighter was being loaded with cotton bales. Under the overhead arc lights the swinging booms and cargo nets cast heavy shadows.

"Do you come down here often, Harry?"

"Every night."

"Why?"

"To look at the ships. As soon as I have my passport I'm going to the United States on a ship."

"How will you get on it?"

"My friend is a boss in the port. He'll find me a job as waiter."

Harry led me to a tarpaper shack set back among oil drums and heavy machinery. Inside, a thick-set Indian was seated at a low table. This was Royes, who would get Harry on a ship to Los Angeles. Another old man squatted next to a charcoal brazier in the corner. I sat down on a box beneath the oil lamp and took a cup of pisco from Royes.

"Royes wants to know if you used to live at the Pensión Americana on Carabaya," said Harry.

"I did, yes."

"He lifts weights at the YMCA. He's seen you there in the courtyard."

While they talked I leaned back against the side of the shack and took a sip of the pisco. The old man had got a pot on the fire and the smell made me hungry. I took out a pack of cigarettes and handed them around. Everyone smoked except the old man, who placed the cigarette behind his ear.

The meal was chicken cooked with *ají* and pieces of cold corn to help kill the heat in your mouth. As he ate, Harry's face glistened with sweat. There were shadows beneath the high cheekbones. From time to time he asked me, *"Está bien? Todo bueno, más?"*

"Sí, Harry, muy bien. Todo bueno."

The shack filled with cigarette smoke and fumes from the charcoal fire until Royes turned around and pushed open the door. With the meal finished the old man took the cigarette from behind his ear and smoked it. I leaned back again as the conversation shifted into their own language. This is the way I'd like to eat every night.

We left so late that I was wondering how we were going to make it back to Lima when I heard a rumble and spotted a row of lights passing through an intersection up ahead. It was the last tram. Harry led me running so fast that we caught up and jumped on. The only other passenger was a Chinaman sitting in back. Harry looked at him and laughed. The Chinaman went on reading his newspaper. Ticket stubs and handbills littered the floor. We sat in silence looking out the window at the empty road whose orange lights illuminated factories and warehouses and junkyards. The trip did not take long, as nobody got on or off. On the way I told Harry that these trams used to run in New York.

Harry could almost always be discovered somewhere around Plaza San Martín. It wasn't long before I found myself wandering down in that direction nearly every night. Being sensitive to everything in the street, he would see me first among the crowds of people and would make his way over to me. We usually went to the cinema or a restaurant, often riding the tram down to Callao late at night to see what new ships were in the harbour. Sometimes we walked around Chinatown, or drank pisco in one of the shingle bars at Mercado Mayorista, or attended a soccer match. Sundays there were bullfights. All this time Harry was sleeping out on the grass of Plaza San Martín, and I could see it wasn't doing him any good. He complained about stiff joints in the morning. One day I bought him a bottle of vitamins to help keep his strength up. That same evening we sat with our feet up against the wire mesh of a cockpit waiting for the fight to begin. He planted his bare arm on the back of the wooden bench as if he wanted to arm wrestle and told me to do the same.

"*Mira.* You're white and I'm brown. That's good."

One morning I encountered him unexpectedly in the street.

The bright sunlight did something to his face. He looked yellower than usual.

"Harry, *qué pasa?* You look sick."

"Sí, estoy enfermo un poco."

"Have you been taking your vitamins?"

He took out the vitamin bottle he always carried with him and listlessly shook it. *"Mira.* Almost empty."

"Take the rest and I'll buy you another bottle. Harry, go to that woman's house and rest for a day. Tell me where it is and I'll come and see you."

He told me the address and shuffled off down the street.

I often called on Sra. Davis, who enjoys my company. She knows something about medicine and I told her about Harry.

"Anybody who lives like that is vulnerable."

"I sleep outside on Bonsal's terrace myself."

"Summer is better. The sun will keep almost anyone alive. Winter is the time when they die."

"He's not afraid of dying. He never thinks about it. His bones ache, but he's more concerned about the grass stains on his suit."

"It might be better if he goes to the United States."

"Isn't there any alternative?"

"If he's sick now you'll have to take care of him. Nobody else will."

I stayed with Sra. Davis most of the afternoon. When I left I hailed the first taxi to come along and gave the driver the address. The man shook his head; he had never heard of it. Even so I rode with him as far as the Plaza de Armas. I had a feeling Harry lived across the Rimac from there. The rest of the day I spent crisscrossing the area without success. Half the streets are unnamed; half the people don't live there. Finally I went into that café-bodega to sit down and rest. By chance the waiter knew Harry and took me to the place. No wonder it had been impossible to find: a dead-end alley with one low door at the end. I pushed it open and entered into a yard where pigs rooted in the dirt. At my appearance two children vanished through the blackened doorway of a house with stones holding down the tin roof. The mother came out, red-eyed from cook smoke. Now I understood why Harry preferred to sleep in parks.

I was allowed to pass through one windowless room into another. A candle was burning in the corner and next to it, on a mat of flattened-out cardboard cartons, lay Harry. With the woman and her children crowding the doorway behind me I went over and knelt down on the dirt floor.

"How do you feel, Harry?"

At the sound of my voice he rolled over. His eyes kept on rolling and I wasn't sure he even knew who it was. He didn't look good to me.

"Harry?"

He opened his mouth and coughed. Whatever had got hold of him, he wasn't putting up much resistance to it. I asked the woman if he had ever been sick like this before and she replied *Sí, mucho.* She and her naked little children looked frightened, as if my presence had brought new seriousness to the situation.

While searching for this place I had passed a brass plaque engraved *médico.* I went out, found it again, and brought the doctor back with me. He didn't like the pigs in the yard and shook his head when he saw Harry there on the floor, but went right to work, thumping the back and chest and listening. Harry lay there inanimate, conscious of nothing. It didn't take long. The doctor snapped his black bag shut and got to his feet. I followed him out into the yard. The pigs had just been given a bucket of garbage.

"Es una pulmonía."

He gave me a prescription and received payment. I stood in the fading light with the piece of paper in my hand and watched him go off, side-stepping the pigs. These South American doctors are all the same: small, bald, anonymous.

I bought the medicine and a handful of candles as well, for I intended to stay with Harry that night. By the time I returned his breath was whistling in and out. I gave him the medicine, covered his body with a blanket from the woman, and sat down on the floor.

After a while I lit another candle. The woman and her children were moving around in the next room. Occasionally one of the little ones put his head through the door. The room was empty. It seemed that Harry had no possessions other than the clothes he wore. On the wall above his cardboard bed he had nailed a single advertisement for an American mattress, cut from a magazine. I had expected that he would have collected all kinds of things. Perhaps he kept them somewhere else.

Gradually all the noises ceased except for the sound of his breathing. Watching that blanket rise and fall, the yellow face with the thick Indian features so insensible, I wondered if he had ever been alive at all, if I had actually talked with him this morning.

Towards midnight I became hungry and went out to the café. The waiter was at the door.

"How is your friend?"

"He has pneumonia."

"Ah. But he's going to get well, no?"

"I don't know."

He brought me a beer and a *pastel de choclo*. It was a warm night. I sat there and listened to the mountain music without feeling anything. When someone is sick, then I become sad.

When I went back Harry seemed improved. His breathing sounded easier. But there was nothing to do except light another candle when the old one burned down, and wait.

I must have dozed off a couple of times but always woke up automatically to give Harry his medicine. He didn't know what was happening. I never saw anyone so visibly give in to sickness. He just lay there and let it run through him. I wondered how he had ever recovered before. A small cheap candle burns down in about an hour, but I had plenty. A rat came around the corner and began to eat one which had rolled over near the door. Its eyes glittered in the candlelight. I could have reached out and grabbed it with my hand, but I didn't. Watching it occupied my attention for a while. After that I fell asleep.

At dawn the people began to move around in the next room. I got to my feet and walked outside. Cold light gleamed from the sun just below the rim of the mountains. The hogs were still in their holes. I drank a cup of coffee down the street and came back. The candle had gone out. Nevertheless, there was enough light to reveal how dirty the place was. Harry lay shivering against the wall. I drew the blanket over him again. He would just die here. I could see that.

"Listen, Harry, this place is no good for you. You can't get well here."

He didn't respond. I shook him.

"Did you hear me, Harry? We're going to get out of here."

I went out and looked up and down the street for a taxi. There was none in sight. I came back again.

"Can you walk, Harry?"

He rolled his cloudy eyes around. The skin was drawn over the cheekbones.

"You're going to have to. Get up."

I dragged him to his feet, propped him up against the wall, and stuffed the medicines into his suit pocket.

"*Vamos.*"

Under my support he made it out to the street. I wanted to guide him to the Plaza de Armas, but he was too weak to walk so far. His breathing suddenly became much worse, and I was afraid I was killing him.

"Are you all right, Harry?"

Gripping his slack body in the middle of the street, I looked about. Some Indians were idly watching us. At the corner I noticed a man asleep in an old Ford. I dragged Harry over and rapped on the window. The man woke up.

"Is this your car?"

"*Sí.*"

I opened the rear door and pushed Harry in. The Indian turned around in his seat, the mouth open.

"My friend is very sick and you must drive us. I'll pay you whatever you want."

A few minutes later we arrived back at the apartment building. There was some trouble with the stairs but we had come so far that I knew Harry would make it. I made him lie down where I usually slept—a bare mattress under the trellis outside —and threw blankets and ponchos over him. When he felt what was underneath him Harry briefly came to life, opening his eyes.

"American mattress?"

"*Sí.*"

Bonsal must have had it there in the sun and fog at least ten years, but the label still told where it came from.

They say Indians don't sweat a great deal, but I've never seen anybody sweat as Harry did during the next week. Olinda, Bonsal's maid, had to wash his suit, wash the ponchos, wash the blankets. I kept turning the mattress over. Harry lay on his back with his eyes shut. Sometimes I used to draw up the chair and watch him. He accepted this sickness with equanimity, as if living and dying were almost the same.

Gradually he began to improve. He heard the beggar's whistle and knew all about the beggar. He'd been a strong man, a stevedore on the docks, who had been run down at that intersection by a truck several years ago. Both legs were amputated. When he was well again he returned to that same corner where the accident had occurred and made his living by begging from the cars that stopped there.

When Harry's fever was down I went around to a carpenter shop and had the man build me a cage. I took it to the Mercado Central and purchased a spider monkey. Harry was delighted. He immediately let it out of the cage. It climbed up on the trellis over his head and lived there. With the same natural quietness as when he was sick, Harry used to watch it happily for hours going through its routine on the trellis.

Harry stayed on at the apartment for two weeks. The first time he went out was to check on his passport. To my surprise he returned with it in his hand. That same night we boarded the tram for Callao. Royes looked at the passport and nodded: he would find Harry a job on a boat to the West Coast. The next day we went to the American Embassy and the visa was granted. It was only a matter of time before the next boat would be sailing north. Of course, I was glad that Harry's dream of going to America was coming true at last, but at the same time I was sorry to see him leave. I felt like those waiters at the hotel up in Tingo Maria.

I was out on the pavement thinking about what I was going to do next when Antonio pulled up in that little English car he uses to commute back and forth to his school in Chaclacayo. Together we drove out to the market. He had received a letter from Paul saying that he would be returning to Peru soon.

"When?"

"He prefers to arrive anonymously."

"There must be some way of knowing."

"He disappears for months into the jungle and then suddenly is seen in Cuzco, down on his hands and knees kissing the ring of the Archbishop in the Plaza de Armas. Then he walks back to Lima."

"I'll move out of the apartment. It's not big enough for more than one person."

"Stay there until he comes."

"He'll want to be alone."

There seemed only one logical place to go. Antonio left me off on Abancay and I walked over to where Anne used to live. The Indian family was seated around their table as usual. The father accompanied me upstairs and stood in the doorway while I looked around the bare room. He said he would ask the old man for permission to rent the tower again.

Out on the street once more I noticed the corner of a brass bed poking out over the wall of a junkyard. I went in and bought it. Three days later I moved into the tower. Harry took the monkey with him to Callao and lived with Royes. I went down there every night. Soon Harry announced, "Royes says a boat is arriving tomorrow bound for the West Coast."

"That's good, Harry, I'm glad."

The next afternoon I put some money into an envelope and headed down to the docks. The ship was already in but I didn't see Harry anywhere. I was standing there among all the loading and unloading when suddenly he appeared up on the superstructure, waving to me. He already had on his white waiter's jacket.

"You've got your job already, Harry?" I shouted.

"I'm on my way to the United States."

I took out the envelope and shook it. "I've got something for you."

"What is it?"

"Come down and see."

He descended to the deck and leaned over the rail. "I'm not allowed to leave the ship."

"That's all right."

I reached up and handed him the envelope. He opened it.

"*Dólares. Gracias.*"

"It's not much."

"I must go back inside now. I'm supposed to be working."

"All right, Harry. *Hasta luego.*"

"*Hasta luego.*"

Nobody ever says *adiós* in this country.

I stepped back from the edge of the pier to get out of the way of the ship's booms. It was a long green ship, a new ship. At that moment Paul Bonsal appeared on deck. He came down the gangplank and walked away with his quick step. When I called his name he seemed surprised, but stepped forward and shook my hand.

"How did you know I was on this ship?"

"I didn't, I just happened to be here."

His hair had grayed considerably since I last saw him.

"My suitcases have been taken to the port entrance."

We piled the suitcases into a taxi and rode back to his apartment. While Bonsal unpacked I stepped out onto the terrace. Callao was still visible, but it was impossible to distinguish Harry's ship from the others in the harbour.

"I see you bought another jug of Ica pisco."

"I did, yes."

He came out through the door with the jug in the crook of his arm. "Best pisco in the world."

He tilted the jug back and took a few swallows. "Take some."

■   ■   ■

About the time the sun goes down I like to drag my chair out on the roof, prop it against the wall, and think how I'm going to establish myself in this country. This is the hour when vultures and sea gulls roost in the old man's trees. Some form of agriculture would be preferable to anything in the city. I'd like to get myself a farm not too far out and work some money crop that in a few years could make a man independent and rich enough to do what he likes. Paul arranged that I see someone called Halito, who knows a good deal about agriculture. He manages a cotton farm about ninety miles south of Lima.

I took the bus and got off at a truck stop in the desert. The barman said Halito came here every night to drink and eat. He rode his horse in from the farm and tied it up among the trucks and buses. I crossed the highway and set out over a rough track through fields of cotton. The soil here was particularly fine and powdery. Dust covered the gray cotton plants. Several dead mules lay beside the road. I noticed they had all been shot. Their carcasses quivered in the heat; swarms of flies rose as I went by. The sun was intense.

Approaching an unpainted frame house I saw a large man sitting in the shade on the high front porch, watching me. I paused at the bottom step to remove my hat and wipe my forehead. He remained motionless in the shadows. This porch was so high and the wood stairs so steep that all I could see was his head peering over the edge. Some insect was making a shrill noise. I put my hat back on.

"Halito?"

"Señor Caffery—I've been expecting you."

I mounted the steps as he descended and we shook hands in the middle. He told me to take a seat at the table and went into the house. On this Spanish table rested a large German pistol with a neat row of bullets laid out beside it. At each end of the row a wooden matchstick had been carefully placed to keep the bullets from rolling away.

"It's plenty hot out here."

"That's right."

He opened two large bottles of beer, shoved one across to me, and sat down.

"I notice your cotton plants are covered with dust. Does cotton grow well in this dry land?"

"The cotton does very well. My truck has thrown some dust

on those plants near the road. There's no rain to wash them off. We irrigate here."

From this position on the porch we could see the whole cotton crop, with the roadhouse off in the distance and the blue sea shimmering behind that. When the insect stopped shrilling, a faint sea breeze brought the sound of the trucks passing on the highway. Heat rose in patterns from the ground, distorting the whole view.

"Quite a number of dead animals lying about."

"I shoot them."

"Why?"

"It's a way of passing the time. There are plenty of stray animals around here that can do a great deal of damage to the crop, particularly the donkeys. They like to take their dust baths, and what with rolling around and kicking out in all directions they can destroy dozens of plants."

"Mules or donkeys?"

"Both. I sit up here on the porch and follow their movements throughout the day. At sunset I have to ride out over the land to open the irrigation ditches. If one of those donkeys is still in the area I shoot it. I've got to keep those stray animals off the land."

He went inside and came out with more beer.

"Two things on this farm I can't live without—my bed and the kerosene refrigerator."

I told him why I had come.

"There's only one answer—cattle fattening."

"What's that?"

"It's a simple operation: buy or rent a few hectares of land, put up fences and feed stalls, get a truck, and go up into the Sierra. Round up as many head of those old skinny cows as you can find, bring them back, and pen them up."

"How do you find these cattle?"

"The Sierra's full of them. Some must be eight or nine years

old. You'd have to look a long time on the Texas range to find a
nine-year-old steer."

"You mean you just grab them while they're wandering
around loose?"

"No, you buy them cheap. Of course, you may come across
one grazing alone by the side of the road which you may just
want to take along with you."

"What do you do with them?"

"Feed them as much as they can take. You just shovel it at
them and they never stop eating. They've had a lean life in the
Sierra. They'll gain as much as four kilos a day, average two or
three. When they're fat and ready, sell them by the kilo to the
Lima market. You'll make a big profit."

"What do they eat?"

"Cottonseed cake or any other available silage. Normally in
two or three months they're ready for the slaughterhouse and
you'll be making money, short term for agriculture."

"It doesn't sound like any agriculture I've ever heard of before."

The long day wore on into the afternoon. I dozed in my
chair. When I awoke Halito was loading the gun. It was time for
the irrigation ditches to be opened. I told him to go ahead without me; I didn't want to shoot any mules. He asked me to meet
him at the roadhouse for dinner. I heard him saddle up behind
the house and ride off. After watching the sun set into the sea I
got to my feet and walked down the dusty road toward the highway. The lights of the roadhouse had been turned on, and you
could see them a long way off across the plain.

This roadhouse had some of the hottest food I ever tasted.
Halito said the Indian truck drivers like it that way to keep
themselves awake during the long hauls. Halito is a big man
himself and eats plenty.

"Señor Caffery, most of my land is useless for cotton. You
can put up your fences a kilometer down the road."

I told him the idea was agreeable to me.

"You can throw down a pipeline from my well with no trouble and feed those cows with the cottonseed cake from the mill in Cañete."

I said I had no money.

"My uncle is a banker. I'll give you a letter and he'll arrange a loan. How does that sound?"

It sounded fine to me. I was ready to begin.

After dinner I got up behind Halito and rode back to the house. He said he would be glad to have me as a neighbour. Out in this desert there was nobody but the truck drivers to talk to. I was so excited about this enterprise that I slept badly that night; besides, I had to sleep on the floor.

The next week was spent in arranging a loan from Halito's uncle. Money is always available in this country, but at a price: this loan was costing me nine per cent annually. With my new bank account I purchased a second-hand red truck, filled it with fence posts and wire, and drove to Halito's farm. His cultivated cotton soil is fine and powdery. But when you have to dig post holes where a plow has never been, the ground seems unbelievably hard. Four men worked with me. Meanwhile I was sleeping at Halito's.

I built a shed for the silage and a roof to protect the cows from the sun. Lumber is expensive but I didn't want them to sweat away any weight they were gaining at my expense. Although I had doubled my estimate of initial outlay when calculating the loan, my actual expenses soon doubled this, and I found myself back at the bank. Halito said not to worry: as soon as the cows began eating, the money would flow the other way. After several weeks the work was nearing completion. With the remaining lumber I put up a shack for myself, in which I installed a bed and a refrigerator. All that remained was to round up the cows.

Two of my Indian workers promised to stay on as cowboys.

Halito suggested a route I might take. So with the pens ready and the shed full of cottonseed cake I rolled a fifty-gallon drum of gasoline onto the truck and threw in ropes, blankets, and two bales of hay. I filled my pockets with money and set off with Manolo, one of the cowboys.

We drove south to Ica, then turned east into the Sierra. Soon we were passing through lush green valleys, intricately terraced and cultivated, and Spanish colonial towns with red tile roofs and old stone bridges over the clear streams. Cows were scarce. We went on higher over twisting roads through bleak canyons and old eroded mountains where nothing grows. This looked to me like lizard country. There must be plenty of them up there crawling out to lie on warm rocks in the sun, watching the lone truck making its way across the valley, raising a rooster tail of dust behind.

The gasoline leaked and soaked the bales of hay. The truck, steadily losing power at the higher altitudes, broke down more than once. Night time Manolo and I rolled up in blankets and slept in the truck as the thin cold wind whistled under the broken floor boards. Finally we reached an altitude where herds of llamas and alpacas drifted across the high plateaus, with snowy peaks in the distance. We'd come too far. We turned back over the difficult roads. Fourth day out I bought my first cow. We had a terrible time getting her up the ramp into the truck, and Manolo dislocated his thumb. This did not seem to give him much pain. He always had a wad of coca leaves and lime in his cheek. I tried it for one day, but it only numbed my mouth and tongue.

At the end of the week we returned to the farm and let the cow loose in the pen. I hung on the fence, waiting for her to eat. She would have to eat a tremendous amount before she would be worth the amount I'd spent on her in gasoline alone.

One day a man rode out of the hills driving ten lean cows before him. I bought the cows, without asking any questions about where he got them, and hired the man. He called himself Vanegas. He was a half-Indian about fifty, and wore leather pants and a belt studded with silver coins. He looked experienced and spoke as if he knew something about cattle. I didn't like the long sharp knife stuck in his belt, but he said he'd used it to take the hides off cows and sheep in Argentina. Halito confirmed that he spoke with an Argentine accent.

There was nothing to do but to set out again in search of more cows. This time I kept to the coast and picked up five in three days. I began making regular contacts around the countryside and soon had thirty cows in the pen. I leaned on the fence watching them. They ate slowly, steadily, all day long, day after day. It was a pleasure to see their bones gradually disappearing. Vanegas gave the sick ones injections, cleaned out their sores, and looked after the new calves. Meanwhile, summer was coming to an end.

■ ■ ■

The shack had only a dirt floor, and I slept with a hammer under my cot to kill the scorpions. Whenever I went north of Lima looking for cows I always tried to spend the night in the tower, which was more comfortable, and to see Bonsal. My enterprise interested him. When I decided to cross over the Andes to the Chanchamayo district in the jungle looking for a big cattle supply, he came along with me.

The stretch of road from La Oroya down to Chanchamayo on the other side of the Andes is one of the most dangerous I've seen. My tires, worn down from the long travels, slipped easily on the icy parts. The cliff falls away hundreds of feet on one side. Wood crosses and flowers indicate where vehicles have gone over and people have died; in the ravine are the burnt-out wrecks of those vehicles. Landslides occur daily in the area. Gangs of Indians worked to clear away the mud and rocks. As we went by, the Indians paused in their work and watched us, the damp cold wind whipping up their ponchos and ear flaps.

In the late afternoon we pulled into La Merced, one of the towns in the Chanchamayo area, and found a high-ceiling room in the San Felipe Hotel. While I was taking a siesta three shots rang out in the street. I went to the window. As usual loud music plays everywhere, bright-coloured trucks and converted buses roar along the dusty main street. Boys sell mangoes and fresh orange juice. Beyond the irregular tin roofs of the town, the forested hills are cross-patched with light green squares indicating cultivation. Smoke rises where new land is being cleared. This is one of the most important agricultural areas east of the Andes, producing coffee and oranges. Now the sun was lowering, and the hills were going from green to blue.

Later we got into the truck and drove to a large German *finca* outside town. One of the tall blond sons showed us around. The farm was an efficiently run establishment of long standing with its own mill for processing the green coffee beans. Under the steps of their big Nyasaland house was a tank of raw rum made from sugar cane grown on the farm. It was Saturday night and the workers stood quietly in the shadows of the house, waiting with bottles and tin cans for their weekly ration. We ate dinner on one of the wide verandas with numerous members of the family. Every one of them had malaria. As we ate, a great deal of noise carried from the Indian shacks among the trees. I looked at Paul across the table, and felt he wanted to be out there with them. As the son poured a small amount of rum into our tea, the father informed me that little possibility existed of finding any suitable stock to transport over the mountains.

When it came time to leave there was a disturbance outside as several drunken Indians attempted to break into the rum tank and were turned away by the foreman. One of the sons was now shouting at them. As I swung the truck around, the headlights illuminated the heavy swollen faces. Paul remarked that the Germans used this rum as a cheap form of payment. The

Indian labourers always wanted it, but never got as much as they wanted.

The night was hot and sultry. I lay in my bed at the San Felipe worrying about malaria. Paul sat by the open window.

"Paul, I didn't like the look of all those yellow Germans."

"They've been here so long they don't know how to take care of themselves."

"They know how to run a farm."

"I'm not impressed by their industry."

"I thought you admired neat productive farms."

"I can walk among orange and grapefruit trees forever, but the Germans' settlement doesn't interest me."

"You wanted them to give you a crate of oranges."

"A crate of oranges and more of that rum."

Past midnight I heard the sound of voices and running. Paul called me to the window.

"What is it?"

"A fire."

A burning shed was sending up clouds of smoke and sparks into the night air; the flames cast long shadows down the street. We dressed quickly and arrived in time to see the corrugated metal roof curl up and split in the heat before the whole structure collapsed in an explosion of sparks. The Indians standing around laughed and shouted. I looked uneasily at their sweating faces reflected in the light of the flames. Even Bonsal seemed excited by the fire.

"Paul, do you think they started this fire?"

"Of course."

Suddenly a group of Indians got behind a parked truck and pushed it into the inferno. It caught fire immediately and I had to drag Paul back to escape the exploding gasoline tank, which sent flaming pieces in all directions. The Indians responded with another yell.

"Paul, let's get out of here!"

He shook me off. At the sound of my voice the Indians seemed to notice us for the first time, but most of them were busy rolling another truck towards the flames. My own was parked not far away. I ran down the street, my long shadow before me. Two Indians were already on the truck. I grabbed hold of the first one, threw him to the ground, and attempted to drag the other out of the cab. However, he hung on to the steering wheel and I couldn't tear him loose. Meanwhile the first seized me around the waist, so I had to deal with them both. It was like fighting with children. Then I caught sight of Bonsal standing by, watching the fight.

"Help me, Paul! My pistol's in here!"

He suddenly lunged forward, pulled the Indian off me, and hit him so hard in the face that he fell down right under the truck and didn't move. I finally succeeded in dragging the other from the cab. Paul caught him and punched him in the throat. The man collapsed across the body of his friend. Now I had the gun in my hand as others approached. Paul plunged into them and was nearly shot by me as I fired over their heads. Paul had one, another turned and ran. I almost shot him down in the street but controlled myself. Paul held his man up against the truck with his left hand and was hitting his face with his right. The Indian offered no resistance and finally just dropped down into a sitting position by the wheel.

By now several buildings were burning with a noise like empty oil drums. Blazing chickens ran across the road with Indians after them. As I watched, the figure of a policeman appeared against the flames. The Indians left off pushing another truck and scattered. Fortunately, the burning buildings were set apart from the rest of the town, so the flames did not spread. In another hour only mounds of glowing coals remained, silhouetting the shells of the burnt-out trucks. I finally got Paul back to the hotel and had a look at his hands. The knuckles were cut. All that night there was running and shouting in the streets.

The next day Paul found his crate of oranges in the market and a sack of coffee besides. I made a half-hearted attempt to locate some cows, but really I was anxious to start back. Although I didn't look forward to passing over those mountain roads in darkness, anything was better than spending another night at the San Felipe. Our room was full of mosquitoes. In the late afternoon we drove out of La Merced past the still smoking remains of the houses and trucks.

The road rises steeply into the Sierra. I stopped sweating and began shivering. Night fell, and Paul covered himself with a blanket. I had my poncho but was never warm enough. As the truck rounded curves the headlights swept out into the darkness. It's better not to see those deep ravines.

Large wet flakes began to stream into the headlights. Paul was slumped heavily against the door, looking like Manolo. My bare arms on the steering wheel received the green glow of the dash light. The snowflakes became smaller and stuck to the windshield.

We caught up to a long convoy of trucks. The soft serpentine of their lights wound slowly up towards the pass. Paul stirred.

"It's too cold to sleep."

"You wish you were back in La Merced?"

"I hated that place."

"Paul, did you want to see this truck burn last night?"

"No."

"I looked at your face when they rolled the first truck into the fire. You were glad."

"I was excited by the fire, and I wanted to see how far they dared carry the riot."

"You almost waited too long."

"I found something natural about that outbreak—setting fire to sheds and trucks, cheering when the gas tanks exploded. Like fireworks. I didn't want to interfere."

"I was fascinated but scared."

"I wanted to cheer—I think I did yell, but when those flaming bits came raining down, suddenly I became very sad."

"Why?"

"Because it was such a futile form of rebellion. But right. They're good people and they resent their existence. But I've known that a long time."

Just below the pass we had a puncture. I climbed out into the storm. The cold was so intense that I jumped up and down beating my sides with my arms to warm myself. Almost immediately I fell down on the road in a kind of faint. Paul dragged me back into the cab and changed the tire himself while I recovered. We never saw the convoy again.

After midnight we reached La Oroya. Paul led me down a narrow side street to a bar, where I took a hot cup of tea between my hands.

"I'm glad you helped me out. I'm fond of that truck, old and rattling as it is."

"Sometimes you have to defend yourself."

"Without that truck the farm would fold. I couldn't round up any more cows. That's what I was thinking when I ran up the street last night—if they get to my truck, no more cows."

After La Oroya we jolted down through warmer layers of air. The windshield unfroze. I was able to open the front vent. It would be good to arrive back on flat land again.

In misting six a.m. light we trailed through the slick cobblestone streets of the capital.

"Caffery, I have to admit that I was hoping they would push all the trucks into the fire, including yours."

"I'm glad they didn't."

"But when you yelled for help, that erased everything."

■ ■ ■

Paul wished to accompany me to the farm. We left late, had dinner at the roadhouse, and installed another cot in the shack.

I gave the place a good searching for scorpions. Paul set out some water for them, said all they wanted was a drink. Nevertheless, I put the hammer and flashlight between us for the night.

With the returning winter came the mist. Stepping outside in the early mornings, one could only hear the cows eating and moving around beyond the dim outline of the fence. However, it normally burned off in a few hours and we had sunny afternoons. The evenings became quite cool and the shack was damp for sleeping. I can't say it was very healthy living out there in winter, but the farm was running smoothly. The herd had increased to nearly sixty head. The condition of each cow perceptibly improved from day to day, and I frequently checked their weight with a complicated secondhand cow scale I had found in Lima.

I put Vanegas in charge of everything. He was a taciturn sort of man, the eyes slightly glazed from the cane alcohol he drank, but he was extremely effective in handling the cattle. Some of these cows arrived from the Sierra half dead. He would talk to them, coax them to eat, and soon they were growing fat like the others. When a cow that had just given birth died, Paul and I watched him take out that long knife of his, straddle the animal, and have the hide off it in a few minutes. Giving us a big yellow-toothed grin he paused to rub the blade across the small stone he always carried.

Paul put out his hand. "Vanegas, let me see that knife."

Vanegas took a step backward and shook his head. "*No, señor*. To touch the knife of another man brings bad luck."

Soon the whole carcass was cut up and hanging from the rafters in the shed. I noticed there wasn't one sign of fat anywhere on the meat. I let Vanegas sell it at the local market at Cañete. He took that sickly calf into the shed and fed it milk from a spoon. The calf survived, and I felt confident that Vanegas was capable of dealing with any situation that arose on the farm.

When he wasn't helping with the work Paul took long walks up into the hills or out to the beach for a swim. He swims year round: to him it doesn't matter how cold the air or water is. Each night we walked over to the roadhouse and had dinner, often with Halito. I spent much of my time sitting on the fence watching the cows eat. This life was not unsatisfactory. My days had assumed a certain order around the work to be done on the farm, which seemed to be headed for a financial success as Halito had predicted. But with my daily activity so established I found myself recalling the time I lived at the Pensión Americana, when I used to walk the streets and wonder what I was going to do.

One afternoon I was in the shack, trimming the lantern wick and figuring roughly how much money I could make on the first lot of cows to be sold soon. Paul came in carrying the thick short body of a snake.

"Where did you find that?"

"Out in the hills. I almost stepped on it."

"You're lucky it didn't bite you."

"I fell over backwards trying to avoid it, but the snake never moved."

"The weather must be too cold for them now."

"I stunned it with my stick, then killed it."

"Let me see."

He handed over the dull brown snake with dark concentric squares along the back. It had a thin neck and large flat head. To me it looked like a fat rattlesnake without rattles.

"On my way back here I heard a gunshot. Halito was riding a horse at a full gallop through the cotton, raising a big cloud of dust."

"He's probably trampled away half his crop by now."

I gave Paul my knife. He cut off the snake's mutilated head and made a slit along the belly.

"Paul, what do you think of this farm?"

"It's fine, but I don't think you'll want to stay out here forever."

"This life can be so monotonous—lying in this shack at night and listening for sounds when there aren't any, switching on the flashlight and hammering a scorpion."

Gripping the skin in his teeth, he cut the flesh away.

"Every day is the same—getting up in the morning and waiting for the fog to burn off to get some work done, then working in the sun."

He stretched the skin over a board, tacked it down, and placed it outside to dry. "Caffery, you knew all this before you started. At least you're supporting yourself and you're in contact with the land."

That, I thought, was about all.

Paul intended to take the night bus back to Lima, so we went up early to the roadhouse in order to have plenty of time to eat. He walked ahead carrying the suitcase, his boots raising light dust from the powdery soil. The crescent sand dunes along the road cast long shadows.

"I suppose your oranges are all rotten by now."

"Olinda takes care of them, sorts the bad ones out."

Suddenly he stopped. "Do you want a scorpion? I just saw one go into its hole."

He put down the suitcase, found a bit of straw of which he wetted one end with saliva, went down on his knees, and eased the straw into a small hole under a tuft of weed. "You have to proceed slowly; the passage twists to prevent such intrusions."

He pressed in the straw until his fingertips reached the entrance. "Now he has it in his pincers; I can feel him."

Very slowly he began to draw the straw out. "If I pull too fast he'll let go."

Paul eased the straw along until the scorpion's claws were visible at the entrance to its hole. Then he pulled the straw sharply out, and with it a large russet scorpion. Immediately the segmented tail went up but Paul clapped his hat over it. "Give me your knife and I'll disarm it."

I passed him my Swiss knife, from which he drew the scissors. He raised the hat and, as the scorpion made a dash for safety, cleverly trapped it under the flat brim, gently enough not to crush it. Only the tail was exposed. He snipped off the stinger with the scissors.

"What are you going to do with it?"

"I'll take it with me to Lima."

He buttoned it into his shirt pocket and we walked on to the roadhouse. During dinner he released it on the table. It hid under the edge of my soup plate. When the waiter took it away he let out a yell and dropped the plate, crushing the scorpion as it fled across the table. That was the end of the scorpion.

The bus pulled out and disappeared into the heavy fog. I was sorry to see Paul go. Living out here on the farm was more pleasant with him around. Otherwise it consisted of the flimsy shack and fences with a great amount of open land and not much else. Hard work kept one busy and often the sky and land would crystallize and take on great beauty, but finally too much solitude prevailed.

I trudged down the highway to the farm. Vanegas had a lantern going in the shed. I found him sitting on a stool repairing his saddle. A pot was steaming on a brass oil burner. Behind him the calf lay on the straw.

"*Buenas noches, señor.*" The ends of his thick mustache moved when he talked.

"What are you cooking there, Vanegas?"

"Like always, fish and beans."

I sat down on his wooden bench. He turned off the flame and offered the pot to me. "Want some?"

"*No, gracias.*"

He found a metal spoon and ate rapidly, chewing with his mouth open. When he finished I gave him a cigarette and we both smoked.

"Those cows will be ready soon."

"*Sí, señor*. They are very fat now."

He reached around behind him for a bottle of clear liquid which I thought was fuel for the stove. He held it out to me.

"What's that?"

"Alcohol."

I took a sip and handed it back. It was terrible strong stuff. He took a long drink and wiped his mouth. That seemed to make him feel better. He picked up the saddle and continued to repair it with thick needle and thread. I pulled my knife from my pocket, flicked out the awl, and handed it to him.

Vanegas examined the knife carefully, nodding his head at each blade. The polished coins on his belt glittered in the lantern light. For a while we sat in silence as he used the awl on the saddle, pausing frequently to drink at the bottle.

"Vanegas, why is it bad luck to touch another man's knife?"

"This? This is not a knife."

He patted the long sheath at his side. There was something wild about him now. The alcohol had dissolved the veneer of mildness.

"What if someone touches that knife?"

"Nobody can touch this knife, *señor*. Very bad luck."

He finished with the awl and returned my knife. Something was happening to his eyes.

"Vanegas, that alcohol is no good for you. Where do you get it?"

He went on sewing with unsteady hands. The lantern showed the deep lines in his face. He seemed such a lonely man, drinking that raw alcohol every night, that I didn't ask him any more questions.

Within a few days Vanegas had the cows ready for shipment to the city. His gentle manner enabled us to weigh and load them into the truck without difficulty. We gave them plenty of feed in case they wanted to eat on the road, and I drove off to Lima. At the end of the trip the cows were unloaded and placed in a pen outside the slaughterhouse. The man who bought them wrote me out a check on the hood of the truck.

Paul was out of town so I went around to see Sra. Davis. She brought me a bowl of red *gazpacho* and listened to me talk about the farm.

"You're always moving around. I need a change, too. I want to find another apartment."

I was exhausted and told her she was better off where she was.

"When I arrived here more than twenty years ago the tailor above my bedroom disturbed me. The tailor died but the son of the tailor continues to disturb me. He works on Saturdays besides."

I remarked that she couldn't find a flat with a better location.

"*Es verdad.* But I would like a view of the sea. All my windows face into that narrow courtyard."

"Señora, in a flat seaport town like Lima there are no views of the sea."

"You travel everywhere in your red truck, but you want me to stay where I am and provide you with *tapas.* I have never left this city. Why do you always object if I want to travel or desire a view of the sea? Paul Bonsal's flat has a beautiful view, no?"

"That's true. I'd forgotten."

"I will look for a new flat."

iv

We trailed a concierge up three long flights of a darkened stair-well. He struck a match before the lock, revealing short spatular fingers that looked as if they had all been amputated in the middle. The door opened into an unfurnished room. The walls reflected the gray afternoon light let in through a window overlooking building tops cluttered with shacks and chicken coops, dead-end streets, and dusty parade grounds.

Sra. Davis pointed her finger at the ceiling. Someone was moving heavily about on the floor above.

"I prefer my tailor."

A vulture glided past the window and landed with a hop on the rooftop across the street.

"They're all the same, señora. Let's go."

It had become clear to me that apartment hunting, like buying records or teaching at the Embassy, was simply her excuse to get out and walk. My legs were dead from climbing stairs.

"*Vamonos.*"

As we went out the vulture was perched atop a mud wall regarding the chickens with a red eye.

Out on the pavement I told her I'd seen enough apartments. Hers was preferable to any of them.

"Es verdad."

"You better stay where you are."

"I'll give a party to show my friends I haven't moved. We'll throw the house through the window."

I made a special trip to Lima for the party and arrived at Sra. Davis' flat to find all her friends seated around the table. There was Paul, looking comfortable, Antonio and a young friend of his, Eduardito, only fifteen years old, who had run away from his family in Arequipa to join his grandmother in the capital, and another friend, Samuel, who had left school and was now looking for a job in the big city. As Sra. Davis served up drinks we took turns in complimenting her on the decision to remain in this apartment. Paul suggested we all have lunch in the garden of Rosita Rios, since it was a Sunday afternoon.

Rosita Rios is located under one of the hills that ring the city, and the smell from the surrounding slums is strong. It was already crowded but they gave us a big table under a grapevine. Indian music plays constantly. Paul did the ordering. First we had *chupe de camarones,* with big red crayfish hanging over the edge of the bowl. Next they brought *anticuchos* with green pepper sauce and stacks of cold corn and cold sweet potatoes to kill the pain. The sun and *ají* made us sweat, and we had jugs of fresh beer and *chicha morada* to keep ourselves cool.

The sad Indian music produced an irresistible elation among the eaters. Some people did a dance with handkerchiefs. Others seemed transfixed by their own slow monotonous hand-clapping. None of us danced. At first Sra. Davis spoke Spanish so fast that I couldn't understand anything, but gradually she slowed down, nodded with the music, and seemed to go to sleep. I felt this music and our company were breaking down in her the tension produced by solitude and boredom. The two boys at the end of the table shouted and laughed and became quiet. After the meal Paul drained down glass after glass of pisco. His friend Antonio put his hand on his shoulder, advising him to go easy as his liver was already in a very bad condition, but Paul went on drinking and drumming his fingers on the table in time to the music. After a while everyone was drunk.

We didn't get out of there until after dark. Leaving the others, I walked through the slick streets back to the tower. The truck was parked outside. I climbed in and was soon out on the highway. Patches of fog lay across the road and I had to go slowly. When I drove up to the farm, the cows blinked through the fence at the yellow truck lights.

In the morning I found Vanegas asleep in the shed. When I gave him a kick he sprang to his feet, his eyes dilated and wild. It was plain that in my absence he had done some heavy drinking. Nevertheless, there was work to be done, and I told him to get to it. His face twisted. "*Mierda!* I'll work when I feel like it!"

I already had a headache from my own drinking. For the second time I ordered him to work or get out, and left him. Suddenly Vanegas came out of the shed after me, this time with the knife in his hand. He was screaming in some incomprehensible Spanish of which I caught that he would kill me for insulting him. I repeated the order and retreated into the shack to take some aspirin and control myself.

The alcohol must have made him like that. Paul said that kind of alcohol is used as fuel for stoves and lanterns. In this drunken state Vanegas might even attempt to carry out his threat. I had removed the pistol from the truck while it was parked in Lima and had left it in the tower. So with the exception of my pocket knife I was without a weapon. And the door to the shack had no lock. I opened it a crack. The mist was still heavy. He had returned to his bench in the shed and was feeding the calf and talking to himself. At this moment Manolo walked past. I called him into the shack and told him to get into the truck and drive over to Señor Halito's farm and bring him back with a gun.

The truck was equidistant between the shack and the shed. When Manolo walked calmly towards it Vanegas stepped out of the shed, warning Manolo not to leave. The knife was still in its sheath. Manolo reached the truck first, climbed in, and shut the door. Vanegas ran forward screaming. Luckily the truck started on the first try; usually it takes some time for the cold motor to turn over in the morning. Vanegas shrieked and threw himself in front of the truck. Manolo, being a gentle Indian and not wanting to run him down, started up slowly, allowing Vanegas to leap up onto the hood. Now Manolo accelerated away, weaving back and forth in an attempt to throw him off. This he finally did, and as Vanegas fell heavily to the ground the knife flew out of its sheath. I'd been running along behind in case there was trouble and made a dive for the knife in the dust just as Vanegas reached for it. His hand fell short, I snatched it up, and we jumped to our feet together. The truck jolted off toward the highway.

Vanegas demanded the return of the knife. When I refused he went into such a tantrum that I was only thankful that I was the one who had the knife. He shrieked that he had been dishonoured and threatened to kill me. The eyes swelled, the cords in the neck became taut, the noises whistling between those big yellow teeth were unrecognizable. I admit I was scared. Suddenly he fell to his knees and begged the return of the knife. I refused again. He hammered the ground with his fists, raising the light dust. There were tears in his eyes. All this time I was pleading with him.

"*Por favor,* Vanegas, calm yourself. You shouldn't drink that alcohol. It's for stoves."

"I want my knife!"

"I'll give you my red knife, the one with all the blades. You can repair your saddle."

"No! My knife! My knife! Give it!"

His brown arms were wet with saliva.

"Vanegas, you can have your knife later, when you feel better."

This seemed to have an effect. He calmed down somewhat and I persuaded him to return to the shed. I re-entered the shack, shut the door, and threw the knife in the corner. Perhaps he'll forget about it. I lay down on the bed and took another aspirin with cold water from the refrigerator. I'm lucky to have this icebox out here. I couldn't get along without it. After a moment I got up and opened the door. He wasn't in sight but I heard the rattle of harnesses and tools in the shed. He was making a search for something. I had time for another glass of water and frantically made my own search for a weapon. Had there been a lock on the door I would have shut myself in to wait for Manolo and Halito while he bombarded the shack with rocks. Now there was no choice but to meet him outside in the open. As Vanegas approached the shack, I picked up Paul's walking stick and stepped outside. I wish Paul were here now.

He'd found some contraption I hadn't seen before. It was a metal bar with two heavy weights attached to one end by chains. He'd taken it off the cow scale. I held the stick out to keep him at a distance.

"Vanegas, what's that?"

"Where's my knife?"

"You took that off the cow scale. You see what alcohol makes you do? You break things. Now we can't weigh the cows. We won't know when they're ready to send to Lima."

"I want my knife!"

"Later, I said!"

"Now!"

He stepped forward and swung the bar at me. I ducked and the chains rattled over my head. When he saw he had missed he went into another fit. His eyes rolled up so only the whites showed; he uttered the most horrible noises, like an animal; there was foam on his lips. When this subsided he took more

long heavy swipes at me, which I easily avoided, always careful
to keep myself between him and the shack. I feared that knife
more than this cumbersome weapon. After each swing I could
have knocked him over the head with the stick but refrained,
preferring to wait for Halito. They were a long time in coming.
The sun had come out hot now and I wanted another drink. As
Vanegas exhausted himself through his fits and efforts with the
metal bar I kept jabbering at him. "Vanegas, *por favor,* it's no
good out here in the hot sun. Go lie down in the shed. It's cool
in there."

"*No, señor.* I thought you were a good man, but you have
kicked me, taken my knife, and dishonoured me."

"I'll give your knife back later. Go have a drink. There is
cool water in your jug. Drink your whiskey, if you like. We're
both thirsty."

At this moment the truck thundered up in a cloud of dust.
Vanegas took another half-hearted swipe at me, his last. Halito
jumped out, his pistol drawn. He had grown a beard. He ran
forward, pointing the gun at Vanegas.

"Halito, hold your fire!" I shouted.

He looked disappointed but put his gun away, and the three
of us easily overpowered Vanegas and made him sit on the
ground. It was decided to take him to the police in Cañete. He
squeezed into the front seat of the truck between Halito and
myself. I drove slowly, more anxious about Halito's pistol than
about Vanegas, who now seemed resigned. The police put him
into jail. I drove back and spent the rest of the day trying to get
some sleep.

The following morning I returned to Cañete to find out what
they proposed to do with him. To my surprise he had already
been released because he hadn't done anything. At first I was
indignant, fearing that he would seek me out once more in revenge; however, as I left the police station there he was, leaning
against the truck, smoking a cigarette. He seemed his mild self

again and only asked to be driven back to the farm that he might collect his horse and possessions. I tried to talk to him on the way but got no response.

When he was saddled up and ready to go I came forward to offer him my Swiss knife.

"I want my knife, not this!" He batted the red knife out of my hand.

I picked it up. "Vanegas, you threatened me with that knife. You wanted to kill me. I'll keep it now."

"*Señor,* you gave your word!"

He jumped on his horse and rode off toward the highway. Bolivar and Manolo came out of the shed. The three of us watched him go.

For the next few days I kept myself busy on the farm. It was a mistake not to have returned him his knife, for he could easily find another. After a while, however, it didn't look as if he were coming back, and the tension eased off. Leaving Bolivar to look after the farm, Manolo and I took another load of cows to Lima.

We stayed away two days and two nights, during which time I bought six more cows and retrieved my pistol from the tower. With this under the seat I felt better during the return trip. Perhaps we'd seen the last of Vanegas.

The farm is situated about one mile back from the main highway. As we approached over the rough track, I sensed something was wrong. Suddenly Bolivar ran out of the shed, waving his arms wildly. I jumped down from the truck and looked at the pens. All the cows were dead.

Vanegas had returned, terrorized Bolivar, torn the shack apart until he found his knife, leapt the fence, and had run like a wolf through the herd, cutting the throats of all twenty-one animals. He had ridden away less than an hour ago.

I opened the gate and walked out among the dead cows.

Twisted into awkward positions, they lay in their separate pools of blood. Where the blood had not yet dried and caked with the light dusk it appeared bright in the afternoon sun. They had put up no more resistance to him than they would have to the butcher's assistant at the slaughterhouse, the one with the gas-pellet gun. Death had been slower, however. There were trails of blood all over the yard where the animals had run wildly about after being cut. The ground where they fell bore the marks of their last spasmodic kicking. One had run headlong into the fence, caught its horns in the wire, and died there, the long tongue protruding. Even Vanegas' bootmarks were visible where he had dashed among them. To me it seemed a sorry way to revenge, this kind of useless slaughter, and I was surprised at him. Now the flies were beginning to settle on the bloody animals. A vulture shadow slipped over the yard.

Without knowing what I would do if I caught up with him, I got into the truck and drove off in the direction Bolívar indicated he'd taken. After several miles of rough riding the terrain became cluttered with red boulders; it was impossible to continue. I left the truck and climbed a low hill covered with sharp reddish rocks. This must be the hill where Paul killed that snake. I'll have to keep my eyes open for them hiding among the rocks. Reaching the summit, I sighted Vanegas about a mile away, riding slowly up the slope of a ridge. I put my hands to my mouth and shouted his name. The noise went rolling away among the boulders, but he didn't seem to hear. I fired the pistol into the air. The report rebounded through the slate outcroppings and orange hills and turned Vanegas around in the saddle just as he reached the top of the ridge. I shouted his name once more, hoping he would hear the sound of my voice. He stopped his horse and was sitting there looking back at me with ranges of hills rising behind him. For some minutes we watched each other across that silent space with the heat coming down out of the sky and the stony earth throwing it back. Then he spurred his horse and disappeared down the other side of the ridge. I emptied the pistol after him.

I turned and walked a few yards across the hill and sat down on a stone. From here the farm seemed insignificant in such a wide landscape—just a transient camp among so much sand and stillness. I picked up one of the sharpened red rocks and threw it away. It rattled down the hill with a hard metallic sound. I wonder where Vanegas will go now—probably back to that part of the Sierra whence he came. I liked that man, and I hated to see him go off like that, no matter what he'd done. There's no question of his becoming lost out there. He's travelled back and forth across that desert many times. I raised the pistol and sniffed at the burnt gunpowder. Land can shape a man. Here, where the land is so immense and unmanageable, sadness seems to be the natural result, or bitterness.

Now above the lumps of dead cattle a great spiral of birds concentrated. I got up and walked slowly down the hill, my boots scuffing against the jagged stone edges.

Bolivar and Manolo had already begun the butchering of the animals. Their work was clumsy, and I wished Vanegas were here that we might follow his example. Halito soon joined us, and we laboured under the diving vulture shadows. The fattest animals were cut up, the others dragged out of the enclosure by hand, then towed some distance away by truck and left. Upon these the birds quickly descended. Vanegas had not neglected the calf. Its blood clotted on the straw. Although hard at work until long after dark, I felt a listlessness coming over me. I didn't have the energy to eat, or to take my clothes off to sleep, or to repair the shack. Vanegas had even turned over the refrigerator.

For the next days there was a glut of meat on the village market. But I didn't bother to count the money in my pocket. The vultures departed, leaving white bones scattered on the dry soil. Meanwhile I lay in the shack wondering what to do next.

One night when it was impossible to shut my eyes I went outside to investigate a noise. A large bird, an owl or hawk, had perched on the fence and flew away at my approach. I looked up at the old moon and listened for the faint sound of breakers borne by the wind. Swirls of dust danced around the yard. A truck was passing along the highway. I watched until its lights disappeared and went back into the shack to put on my boots and jacket. I stepped outside again and set out over the land to the north. My eyes soon grew accustomed to the darkness. The wind picked up and blew the dust away from my footsteps. After a few minutes I stopped to look back. The shack and shed were small dark shapes in the moonlight. Black hills rose to the east. In an hour I skirted a stand of corn rustling in the wind and entered the low cotton. My boots sunk deeply into the fine powdery soil. A noise on my right stopped me short; my eyes made out the form of a donkey moving through the cotton. Finally I came out onto the dirt track and walked up to the house. At the bottom of the steep steps I waited to catch my breath; then I shouted, "Halito! Halito, are you in there?"

There were grunts and noises of bedsprings, then of bare feet padding on the wood floor. A light flickered and he appeared on the porch holding a lantern out before him.

"Who's that? Caffery?"

"Yes."

"What's the trouble? Has Vanegas come back again?"

"No, he hasn't come back. Everything's all right. Halito, I've had enough of the farm."

"What do you mean? Are you going to leave?"

"That's right."

"When?"

"As soon as I can. Do you want to buy what's left?"

He yawned and sat down on the top step. "I'm interested. How much?"

"The first loan from the bank is half paid off. The interest on the second has been settled for one year."

"All right."

"There are six cows eating now, all in good health, and twelve more coming in this week, already paid for. Two tons of cottonseed cake in the shed."

"What about the truck?"

"I just had it repaired. It's running well."

He adjusted the lantern. It was casting shadows over his heavy face. "I like that truck."

"Halito, I want to break even."

He scratched his beard. "All right, Caffery. You leave and I'll take over."

"Thank you, Halito."

"Where are you going, Caffery? Leaving the country?"

"No, just Lima."

"What will you do there?"

"I don't know."

"All right."

I turned and began to walk away. Before leaving the circle of light, I stopped. "Halito!"

"Yes? What?"

"There's a donkey out in the cotton."

"Where?"

"A few hundred yards down the road. I saw him on my way over here."

"All right, Caffery, I'll get him tomorrow."

"Halito!"

"What?"

"Where do all those donkeys come from?"

"They just drift down from the Sierra."

"Oh."

"Do you have any over on your place?"

"None."

"There's nothing for them to eat there."

When I passed by the corn again the donkey had disappeared. I looked back and saw Halito still on the porch with the lantern beside him. In another minute he got to his feet and went inside, and the light was extinguished.

■ ■ ■

The old man who owned the tower had died. The property was being broken up and I had to move out into a cheap hotel. My room was comfortable enough, but the long neon light above the mirror kept flickering after it had been turned off. It was like a luminous mouse running back and forth in the tube. Watching it made me uneasy, and after a few nights I was ready to move again.

Outside the hotel two ragged fishermen in old straw hats, with a box of fish and scales between them, were peddling their catch. Their cries echoed up and down the narrow street. When the people came out of the houses with baskets and frying pans, the fishermen put down the box and set up the scales.

In the afternoon I accompanied Bonsal down to Callao for a swim in the harbour. The water was as cold as ever. We swam quickly out and clambered onto the raft. As we lay there the sun appeared from behind the clouds. In a few minutes it became quite comfortable, and I rolled over on my stomach.

"Paul, I have to find another place to live."

"Why don't you move down here to Callao?"

"All right, but where?"

He pointed to some barges tied to a jetty across the water. "There. I know the old man who takes care of them."

We swam back in, dressed, and walked around to the barges. There were three of them, long narrow hulks that had once carried fish meal. The cabin on the middle barge had been painted bright yellow, with a green and red door. Paul shouted and an old Indian poked his head out the window.

"That's him. *Buenas tardes*."

He recognized Bonsal and came out on deck. He was short and had wide splay feet. They were the widest feet I had ever seen.

"Are these your barges?"

"No."

"My friend has been out on the desert a long time and wants to live near the sea for a while."

The old man nodded.

"Are the cabins on the other barges occupied?"

"No."

"Old man, do you want to rent one of those cabins?"

The old man locked the door of his own cabin, threw down a plank to the next barge, and padded softly across. The other cabin was not in bad condition. There were a bunk, a table, a chair, and a small wood stove. I asked him how much a place like this rented for. He looked down at his big feet and made a price even lower than the pensión. Paul said it was the cheapest place he'd ever heard of. I told the old man I'd take it. His name was Pablo. Before long I was living in the harbour.

The barge rocks imperceptibly throughout the night, so it was good sleeping. The first morning I opened my eyes to see a whole flock of pelicans fly by the window. I lit a fire in the stove to keep off the dampness and stepped out on deck. Down the line a large crane was lifting lumber out of a freighter's hold and dropping it on flatcars. Pablo didn't seem to be around. I locked the door and walked into town for breakfast. I read in a newspaper that an earthquake had destroyed an entire Andean village. It seemed to me that the barge would be a safe place during such a catastrophe, unless a tidal wave followed.

I spent part of the day wandering around the port. The odour of fish meal prevails. I walked from ship to ship past long lines of creosote pilings and thick metal cleats. From the polished rails of clean Scandinavian ships blond pale-eyed boys gaze vacantly out across the brown land to where the Andean foothills rise into the overcast. Sitting along the pier on coils of rope, rusty oil drums, on three-legged chairs tilted back against tar-paper shacks, old men watch the sea with opaque Indian eyes. Sea gulls and pelicans float on the easy swell.

Royes was out there. I told him I was living in the harbour now. He said he didn't know when Harry was coming back.

Except when the stove was red-hot the nearness of the water and succession of cloudy days made the barge too damp for healthy living. The bed sheets never seemed to dry out. I began to wake up with aching joints. Therefore when the sun broke through the clouds one morning I decided to take a long walk along the coast to that beach beyond Herradura. The sun would do me good.

Tramping along I felt rather weak and was perspiring a great deal. Perhaps it was too far to come. Yet by noon I reached the deserted beach laid flat by the winter waves. I took off my clothes and lay down on the warm sand, which would have been comfortable had not a slight breeze been blowing. To escape this I crept behind a low dune and lay on my belly and heaped up the warm sand around me. It became necessary to change my position often to seek more warm sand. I hated that light wind. The sensible thing was to put on my clothes, but they were on the other side of the dune exposed to the wind. Finally I dug a shallow pit for protection. As I dug deeper the sand be-came cooler. I just wanted to bury myself to keep warm. Mean-while the shadows of the dune lengthened toward the pit. At last I was forced to get up and dress myself.

It took me a long time to walk back to Herradura, where I hoped a bus would be waiting. But nobody was around. I went on, feeling very weak and feverish now, and reached Callao after dark. I pounded on Pablo's door to tell him I was sick, but nobody answered. In my own cabin I attempted to light the stove, but gave up and crawled into bed. That night I alternated between chills and fever. I thought I'd caught malaria in Chanchamayo.

All next day I lay in bed watching the pelicans ride the easy swell. There always seems to be a flock of them out there, all facing into the wind. In the evening I went to the window and yelled to Pablo. His window was dark. Across the harbour a ship was being loaded. Its lights were reflected on the oily water. People were moving around. I envied their activity and freedom, but they were all too far away. I was out here on the end of the pier by myself.

It was difficult to say how long I stayed in that bed; with so much grayness the hour never seemed to change. I had some water in a bottle but no food. Soon the water was gone. A dull pain developed under my rib cage on the right side. I had terrible cramps across the back and stomach. During the nights I sweated. The sheets soaked through, the blankets and mattress became damp. I used to throw off the covers in disgust, but in the end drew them gratefully back over me. Something was wrong with my liver; my piss turned the colour of tea. If only Pablo or somebody would come.

I kept asking myself how did I ever get myself like this—so sick and stranded at the same time on the end of a deserted pier? Paul is praying at his monastery in the Sierra, Harry is in Los Angeles, Anne on a farm in Tarapoto.

Other pains developed in my lungs. It hurt to breathe deeply. I must have pneumonia like Harry. I lay back and yelled and yelled for Pablo, but nobody heard. He must have gone away somewhere—back to the Sierra. I think my voice was audible only to myself. Looking carefully through a window for pelicans my vision went wrong. When all became unclear I left the bed and went to the window. A skiff came by, propelled by a man standing in the middle. I waved. He paused in his work at the oars to wave back, and went on.

Any exertion exhausted me. I seemed to be breathing off the

tops of my lungs. Nevertheless, I put on my pants and stepped outside. It was good to be in the open air again. There was some difficulty crossing the plank, but I finally managed it on my hands and knees. Down the pier a ship was moored. The high prow and superstructure cut the evening sky. I progressed from piling to piling, grasping the creosote wood in my hands. It grew dark. Powerful arc lights were turned on. The ship's boom swept a whole netload of orange crates up into the air. The oranges glistened through the wood slats. I'd like to be suspended up there, to peer down through the meshes at the Indian faces. The boom switched and the load descended into the hold. The men were looking at me. Probably they wanted to load the crate on which I was sitting. I got down but stumbled among the heavy ropes and fell forward. Some made an effort to break my fall, others watched curiously.

■ ■ ■

During the long afternoon sleep I used to dream fitfully. I was the spectator watching the neon dice roll down over Plaza San Martín. Llamas drifted across Andean plateaus. On bitter rainy days smoke seeps through thatch roofs into the thin mountain air. Herd boys, crouching in the lee of mud walls, played fragile music on reed pipes. In fluid mosaic amber monkeys slipped through pale tree tops. The branches bent together, following the lines of bright prehensile monkey tails. The monkeys disappeared, the llamas moved off over the *puna,* and I awoke with the residue of sadness.

Paul came to visit and remarked that he had never seen anyone so transformed. During the days alone on the barge I'd lost a good deal of weight and had turned a dull yellow. The greatest danger was the pneumonia, which had almost killed me. But the drugs took hold, allowed me to breathe easy, and I was safe again.

The day they permitted me to leave the clinic I was unsteadily making my way across Plaza San Martín, suitcase in hand, when a shoeshine boy pointed at my boots. I sat down heavily on a bench and told him to go ahead. Looking over at the Hotel Bolivar I wondered if I could afford to recuperate there a few days. Explaining that he had no other colour, the boy was applying red polish. Just then Sr. Alvarado walked by. When I called his name he came over and sat down beside me on the bench. It was good to see him again.

"I've been looking for you, Señor Caffery, but I didn't know where to find you. Señor Caffery, you don't look well."

I told him I'd been living on a barge in the harbour, became seriously ill with hepatitis and pneumonia, and had spent a month in the hospital.

"I was in Tarapoto not long ago and saw a friend of yours."

"Anne."

"I met her briefly in a saloon. You know, she's become interested in cattle farming and asked me about strains of cattle. She wants to import bulls from Texas to improve her stock."

"How do you get a bull into Tarapoto? By raft?"

"By plane, but it's not practical. I suggested she buy sperm for artificial insemination. It's easier and cheaper. I have some friends in Texas who will be able to help her."

"Is she happy up there?"

"She seems to be. Also, I am sending her some avocado seedlings."

"Did she say how long she plans to remain?"

"Indefinitely, I believe. She wants to have her own farm."

Sr. Alvarado took off his wide brim felt hat and creased it. "Señor Caffery, you don't look well at all. I'm leaving for the hacienda tomorrow. If you would like to accompany me, I believe it will be a good place for you to regain your strength."

I gratefully accepted his invitation. He left me feeling the same warmth for him as I had so many months before. It was just chance to have met him here like this, and to have him invite me to his farm. But otherwise I don't know what I would have done.

The boy was seated on his box waiting to be paid.

"Botas rojas?"

The boy nodded. I gave him a coin.

As I got to my feet an old man next to a big wooden camera on a tripod made a sign to me. I went over and he took a picture of me with the suitcase. It required some time for the plate to develop but I wasn't in any hurry.

At the hotel they gave me a large room overlooking the Plaza. I stretched out on the big bed, looked at the photograph, and didn't wake up until after dark. There was a long tub in the bathroom, and I lay down in that for a while, feeling good. Later I went downstairs and mailed the photo to Anne, with a note telling her how sick I'd been. In the bar I met an Italian from Tingo Maria. I can't remember his name, but we played dice and talked about the land. Although the doctor advised me not to touch alcohol, I couldn't resist a couple of pisco sours. I believe they did me good. The Italian said Sàndor had fallen out of a tree and hurt his back. Afterwards I went to a place and had some meat roasted on a charcoal grill. Unfortunately I had to turn down the hot sauce. There didn't seem to be much else to do after that but go to bed. Alvarado would be by early in the morning.

■　■　■

The first days at the hacienda were very restful ones for me. In the morning I generally walked down through the grapevines to the stream that plunged along the base of the rock escarpment at the southern edge of the valley. There I took off my clothes and clung to a boulder under the water, letting the heavy current wash over me. Nearby was a smooth warm rock that had a special depression, worn away when the stream had coursed through a different bed, into which my body fitted perfectly. I lay there and often fell asleep in the sun. About noon I returned to the house by another route, along a row of giant century plants raising their stalks into the clear air, or around the bottom of one of the cotton fields.

After lunch I always took a long siesta and then went out to sling some grain at the peacocks and look at the fighting cocks in their separate cages. Sr. Alvarado rode in from the fields at dusk, mixed up some pisco sours, and we sat out on the veranda. We talked mostly about the farm and agriculture in general as the light faded behind the ridge sloping down to the west. He said I was looking better each day. I told him I was sleeping more deeply than I had in months. The dry desert air was the reason.

One evening he asked me if I felt strong enough to accompany him to the upper valley. He intended to build a dam there to act as a reservoir when no rain fell in the Andes. In the wet season it would control flash floods.

"Do you have floods in this part of the country? I thought it never rained on the coast."

"That's true. It seldom rains here at the farm, but the Andes receive a great deal. Then *huaicos* are common."

"What's that?"

"Mudslides. They often block the stream. Then the river rises behind them and breaks through in a flood. When the level of the river here goes down sharply we know what will happen, but can't do anything about it. But a good dam will control the floods somewhat."

Early the next morning we drove up a dirt road to where the stream courses down from the northern to southern edge of the valley. We were transported across in a wooden box slung beneath a cable. On the other side waited the foreman Maximilian with three horses. He had a long dark beard. We mounted up.

Sr. Alvarado, riding easy and smiling beneath his broad straw hat, explained that the soil here was too rocky for cotton and grapes and pointed out the avocado and pecan trees he had recently planted. I liked to hear Sr. Alvarado talk about his land because he cared so much about it. Gradually the valley drew in. Pale green cacti sprouting yellow and orange Barbary figs gripped the rocks. High up on the cliff a man walked behind a donkey. Maximilian said the trail led to a silver mine back in the mountains.

The actual construction of the dam had not yet begun, but the site had been surveyed and staked out. Now about twenty workmen were attempting to divert the stream. While Sr. Alvarado talked with them Maximilian and I watched the work in progress.

"It doesn't look like a very good place for a dam," I said. "The valley is too wide here."

Maximilian nodded.

After a while we remounted and rode on. Before long the valley narrowed to a gorge through which there was just enough room for the horses to pass beside the plunging stream. From this we ascended out into a rocky ravine half in the shadow cast by the cliffs, half in brilliant sunlight. We had a glimpse of hazy mountain ranges lifting one upon another to the east. Sr. Alvarado dismounted in the shade of a single tree growing out of the rocks. Maximilian went to wash his face in the river.

"Is this the end of your property?"

"No, it extends several more miles upstream, but it's worthless for cultivation. There's nothing but rocks. Señor Caffery, what is your opinion of the dam?"

"There's not much to see."

"I hope it will control erosion. The soil is already thin and I can't afford to have much more of it washed away. And there's always the danger of flash floods pouring down through the hills."

"It's hard to believe that flash floods exist in this land."

"One year the whole upper farm was swept away and two

men drowned in the floods. The dam is designed to arrest them. Unfortunately, the lake behind it will permanently inundate at least two hectares of good land. And now I see that the diversion of the river during construction will cut through another productive field."

"I believe the best way to arrest floods is through a series of dams."

"I know, but I feel that one strong dam will be enough."

"If you're going to build one dam, why don't you build it in this ravine instead of in the cultivated area? Then you won't be wasting any good land."

"We considered this, but the engineer thought the ravine too narrow."

"But it would be much simpler. Extend the dam between these two rock faces. You can build right on this bedrock. There's plenty of good soil in the fields above your present dam site, which in floodtime will be washed down. That lake will eventually silt up. Above here, you say, there's nothing but rocks for miles up the ravine."

"Yes, the *huaicos* occur high up in the Sierra."

Maximilian returned, his long beard dripping with water. Sr. Alvarado had me repeat to him all that I had said.

"*Sí, señor,* but will it be possible to pass by such a dam?"

"Maximilian lives up above here, you know."

"Yes?"

"He's the foreman of the upper farm and has built himself a small house in a canyon not far from here. He has to pass through this ravine to get to his home. He's somewhat of a hermit."

"Then it will be necessary to build a path along one side of the lake. That's not difficult."

"It would be a deep lake between these two cliffs."

"And in summer, Señor Alvarado, when the lake will serve as a reservoir for irrigation, it will not only be deeper but have a smaller surface area, which will lie in the shadow of these cliffs. So you will lose less water through evaporation."

Maximilian nodded. "I think Señor Caffery is an engineer."

"And you won't be wasting any arable land at all."

"There's little enough of it."

"As the stream keeps to the base of that cliff, you can erect three-quarters of the dam on dry rock, divert the stream through a culvert, and build the remainder."

We sat in the shade of the tree for some time discussing the details of construction. The sun beat down heavily and was reflected back by the smooth white stones and quartz chips. Except for our talk and the faint noise of the stream nothing disturbed the silence of the ravine. Beyond, the shadowy mountains wavered in the heat.

Sr. Alvarado seemed excited by the idea of building the dam at this site. "I think that such a lake would provide some good swimming and fishing as well."

"You can stock it."

"Señor Caffery, have you built dams before?"

"Never."

"But you say you know something about engineering?"

"Yes."

"Do you think you can build this one?"

"I think so."

"Then I won't have to rehire that engineer who suggested the original site. But do you feel strong enough to do this job? You haven't been long out of the clinic."

I told him I was still somewhat weak, especially in the legs, but I would take it easy in the beginning.

On the way down the valley Sr. Alvarado ordered the men to suspend work on the dam and begin moving the equipment upstream to the new location. The next day we marked out the exact location of the new dam, which was slightly upstream from where I had suggested, due to certain cracks in the rock.

Work was begun almost immediately. The men cleared away the loose rocks from the strip where we meant to lay the foundations of the dam. Along that line I had them place small charges to blast a shallow trench in the bedrock from which vertical construction would commence. We hid behind boulders during the explosions, which reverberated back and forth between the cliffs. When the dust settled, the rubble was cleared away and new holes drilled for further charges. Before any of this was done, however, I scaled both sides of the ravine with a team of men to make sure that the concussions would not spill boulders down upon us. Often I had to do a little boulder rolling myself where it looked as if an explosion might set one loose on the hillside above the ravine. This I enjoyed a great deal. The way was cleared, we got underneath with crowbars and wedged them free. The boulders went hurtling down and plunged off into the ravine. A shout went forth from the men below if they landed in the deep water of the stream, sending up tremendous geysers.

But mostly it was just plain hard work under the sun. More than once I found myself reeling from dizziness and had to sit down in the shade of the tree. Yet at midday it was possible to go for a swim in the river and have a siesta afterwards. I always looked forward to the long ride down the valley at the end of the day. The western ridge cast a jagged shadow on the opposite hills. The air was pleasantly cool. To me this kind of work made more sense than cattle fattening ever did. At least I was involved here in the construction of a thing of some permanence. I only hoped I was doing this thing right. Sr. Alvarado was taking a chance on me, and I didn't want to build him a dam full of holes, or one that would collapse with the first flood. He used to appear every day to see how the work was getting along. When he was obliged to return to Lima on business, he left me in charge of the whole operation. The men already called me *ingeniero*.

With the initial blasting completed, the trench in the bedrock was shaped by hand to hold the foundations of the dam, slightly concave as viewed from without to better resist the pressure of the water. All work was done manually, as no machinery could be transported over the narrow path that led to the dam site. We didn't need machinery anyhow. Half the twenty men employed worked at shaping with chisels and hammers blocks of stone blasted from the hillside. I don't know where Sr. Alvarado found these men. Apparently most of them came right off the farm and had no previous experience in this kind of work. But they learned quickly. The stone cutters crouched beside their boulders, stone dust on their arms, and worked slowly and steadily. Soon each was turning out per day about two cubic and slightly trapezoidal blocks measuring one-half meter across. These were fitted together as closely as possible with cement. A good many were required, as the dam would be four meters thick at the base, one meter at the top, and more than seven meters in height. The two cliffs were nearly twenty meters apart. It looked to me as if we were going to have a strong dam. I didn't want any of those flash floods washing it away.

At noon, when the men laid off work for lunch and a siesta, I used to walk upstream to a particular clear pool and have a swim. One day some of the stone cutters accompanied me far beyond the pool. The ravine narrowed until it became a vertical slot in the earth, nearly one hundred feet deep. There I was shown a natural bridge of red stone that had remained when the gorge had eroded away. It arched across the chasm far over our heads. The men seemed particularly impressed by it. As we rested in its shadow one of them pointed up at the span and said in broken Spanish, "That's no Inca bridge."

Maximilian used to ride by almost every day and never failed to get down from his horse and sit for a while under the tree. In that position his beard hung nearly to the waist. Even in the heat he always wore a long black coat and looked like a preacher or an enormous bird of prey come to watch. Extremely reticent, he quietly rolled cigarettes between his dirty fingers and listened to me explain what we were doing. His blue eyes glittered under the broad soft-brim hat. Maximilian was Austrian.

By now the culvert had been completed and several levels of blocks were in place along the north face, so that it became necessary to pile up an earth ramp against the dam in order to drag the new blocks up. They were put on simple wooden sleds which required four men to tow.

"That's a sturdy dam you're building," Maximilian remarked.

"I suppose it looks like slave labour to see those Indians hauling that sled and stone up the ramp, but they never complain."

"They know how to work."

"I think they prefer this kind of work to the fields. I keep telling them that what we're erecting here shall last for some time, as long as that natural bridge upriver."

Maximilian nodded.

"Do you see how closely those blocks fit together? They've been given a slightly trapezoidal shape so that the pressure of the lake will lock their surfaces in a horizontal arch."

"I'll be able to get by, won't I?"

"Your path will run along the north side, where the ramp is now."

Maximilian had several times invited me to his house, so one evening when I had worked past sunset, I decided to spend the night near the dam. I was too exhausted for the five-mile ride down the valley to Alvarado's house. When all the workers had departed, I got on my horse and rode up the ravine.

There was some kind of glow in the sky to the east. I thought there must be a fire up in the mountains until the moon rose so suddenly that I gave a start in the saddle. But I was glad to have it. Maximilian had pointed out to me the trail that led to his house, but I wasn't certain I could find it again at night. The moon cast shadows across the dead silence of the land. The horse made its way carefully among the rocks; the grating sound of its hoofs was paced and easy.

I found the trail and climbed up through a dry wash and out across a shallow valley encircled by low ridges. Numbers of century plants grew about, their stalks silhouetted in the moon. I don't know why Maximilian chose to live in such a desolate place, but he'd been around some and knew what he wanted. Anyone who dressed like that is bound to be somewhat eccentric.

When a dog began to bark in the distance I figured the house must not be far away. Soon I sighted it high up in the shadow of a rocky bluff—a low whitewashed structure with one window and an open door and pale lantern light visible through both. As I approached, Maximilian appeared in the doorway. Seeing who it was he threw a stone at the dog and came forward to meet me.

"I was working late and decided to take you up on your invitation."

"You're welcome. Come inside."

The horse was put away and I was led into a low-ceiling room with bare cement floor and fireplace at one end. A lantern burned on a wood table. A green cactus hung over the door, ponchos and snakeskins on the yellow walls. There was a certain heavy odour about the place which reminded me of Sierra Indian huts.

"Please sit down. *Mi casa es tu casa*."

He called into the next room and a young Indian girl appeared with two bottles of beer. She couldn't have been older than sixteen but already had that weary used look about her. I got up from the table and shook her hand. This was the first Indian woman I'd seen without a hat on. She smiled briefly and disappeared again.

Maximilian and I sat at the table and drank the warm beer. "Did you have any difficulty finding your way up here?"

"No. The moon helped."

"Full moon tonight."

"I don't suppose many people come up this way."

"Nobody."

"This is kind of lonely country."

"That's right. I don't mind it."

"Nothing grows. What do you burn in that fireplace?"

"Coal. Sometimes she goes down and carries back a bundle of sticks."

He took out his paper and tobacco and began to roll a cigarette.

"You say there's water up here?"

"A spring. A few years ago I rode up into this valley looking for water and found it."

He handed me a cigarette. I guessed Maximilian to be about forty-five. The heavy beard covered most of his face.

"Most of the rock in this valley is shale. There's always water leaking out of shale."

The girl brought the food to the table. It was a simple meal of peanut soup, sweet potatoes and corn, and some meat in a hot red sauce. I had the corn in my mouth when something began to stomp around on the roof over our heads. I looked up at the ceiling and then across at Maximilian, who was busy eating and paid no attention to the noise. He had to hold on to the end of his beard with one hand to prevent it from separating the soup. Now it sounded as if someone was raking leaves up there. I didn't know whether they kept chickens or turkeys on the roof, but I never heard chickens make a noise like that.

"What's that noise?"

"Pepina is collecting some figs for our dessert."

"What?"

"Wild fig trees grow near the spring. She picks the figs and spreads them out on the roof to dry in the sun. Sometimes she has a hard time finding them in the dark."

Just then there was a sharp scream and a thud.

"What was that?"

"She's fallen off the roof."

We ran outside and found Pepina mixed up with a cactus plant that grew by the side of the house. Maximilian dragged her out. She was whimpering and covered with prickles but otherwise seemed all right. I thought she was lucky to have fallen on the plant; the ground is hard as stone and she might have broken her neck. We helped her search in the moonlight for the dried figs that had tumbled over with her, but with little success. It was almost impossible to distinguish them among all the stones and pebbles. Finally we left her and went back inside to finish the meal.

"She's always breaking down that cactus."

"You mean she's fallen off before?"

"Almost every fig season she manages to stumble over the edge, always seems to land on the same cactus."

A few dried figs were served with a bottle of pisco. This makes a good combination. Maximilian took a long drink, trimmed the lantern, and began to roll more cigarettes. I found him difficult to talk to.

"Maximilian, what's up behind this house?"

"More of the same kind of terrain—a few flat valleys like this one, but mostly eroded land, ravines and ridges."

"Have you been over it?"

"Yes, a few times. I've visited Indian villages you can only reach on foot or horse."

"How far is that?"

Maximilian laid out another cigarette for me on the table. "Not far, but it's frustrating land to travel through. You always seem to be at the bottom of a deep ravine, following a dry stream bed. After a while you want to leave the ravine and scale a hill to see where you're going. But the hill invariably turns out to be a low one. In summer the rocks split in the heat, making a sound like a gunshot. I never got used to it."

Pepina came padding softly through the room.

"But it's worth it if you like that kind of country."

"I do."

"Since I found water and built this house I haven't moved. Pepina appeared, and it seemed sensible, living the way I do, to have an Indian woman with me."

It was late. Maximilian rolled out a straw mat for me on the floor, said goodnight, and took his lantern into the bedroom, shutting the door behind him. I stepped outside to breathe some fresh air and looked down the valley. After a few minutes I went in and rolled myself up in a blanket. My head was propped against the wall near the door and soon I began to hear all the noises Maximilian and Pepina were making in their bed. The noises didn't last very long, however, and I was tired enough to sleep.

■ ■ ■

With the dam more than half completed, work was begun to divert the stream from its bed through the culvert on the opposite side of the ravine. This required blasting a deep channel through solid rock. I had waited until now to do this, thinking that such a channel dividing the construction area might interfere with other work. Donkeys and perhaps men would fall into it, break their legs, and there would be a terrible time getting them out. However, I now discovered my mistake. To detonate a charge of any size in the same bedrock upon which the dam was built would shake the foundations, opening fissures through which water pressure would push leaks as the lake rose. Therefore only extremely small charges could be used. We exploded up to a hundred of these a day, clearing away the rubble and drilling a new hole after each explosion. This tedious process took many days, and many workers sat by idle. After a while the sharp concussions and pungent odours gave me a headache. The dust penetrated the clothes and formed crusts around my nose and eyes. There was grit between my teeth. At midday we had little protection from the heat as the brilliant sunlight fell vertically between the cliffs, reflecting off the white stones.

We were joined by a rather large number of Indians attracted by all the noise. It became a problem to keep them out of the way of flying rock. I don't know where these people come from, probably from those villages Maximilian talked about. They just appear out of a land that seems entirely uninhabited. A few of the men were eventually hired on, but the others just perched all day on the boulders like birds. From the looks on their wide, open faces they obviously enjoyed the show. Finally the channel was opened, the stream diverted, and the construction of the remainder of the dam begun. This routine was less spectacular, and most of the Indians drifted away.

One afternoon late as we sat under the tree Maximilian asked me to go with him to a village fiesta in the Sierra.

"Do we go by horse or on foot?"

"No, this village is on a road. Every year we take all the people from the hacienda."

That was a Sunday with a holiday following. We set off before dawn in Sr. Alvarado's old truck. Maximilian and Pepina sat with me in the cab. In back were more than fifty Indians from the farm. I don't know how they all fitted in there, but off we went, rattling over the dirt roads. We came out onto the coast highway, turned north for about twenty miles, and then headed inland on another track. This happened to be the same road on which Anne and I had been picked up by that bus after spending the night in the Valle de las Culebras. The day heated up. The road sloped steadily upward and became worse, but by noon we were well up into the Sierra. The land was massively eroded, but some rudimentary agriculture was being carried on.

Indians worked with footplows on the steep slopes. I found the mountain air invigorating, but when the wind was behind us came clouds of dust and the smell of sickness from the Indians. Pepina leaned across Maximilian and vomited out the window several times.

Soon we became part of a general migration towards this village. Other trucks loaded with Indians were behind and ahead of us. By the side of the road mostly Indian women shuffled along, all carrying something on their backs, all twirling spindles of wool. At what I thought to be about ten thousand feet we passed some black Andean lakes on the edge of a vast dull red plain with snowy peaks far away. The sky here is dark blue coming on black. Out in the middle of this expanse stands a solitary church. It has the common Spanish colonial façade with double wall belfries silhouetted against the dark sky. This church was the focus of some celebration. Hundreds of tents were pitched on the red soil around it; thousands of Indians were milling about.

The instant I stopped the truck all our Indians jumped down and disappeared into the crowd. There was nothing to do but wander around. I've never seen so many things for sale: yellowish *chicha* foaming out of big clay jugs, tangled sheep's guts draped over crosspieces, shoes made out of old rubber tires, mounds of purple potatoes. It was hot; the sun burns with a special intensity through the thin mountain air. This fiesta must have been going on for some time, for many of the Indians were drunk. The situation was especially chaotic in front of the church, where a large mob had assembled. Some were trying to get in, others out; so there was plenty of dull pushing and shoving. Incense was strong; babies cried. It's the women who are most violent in a crowd.

I spied some boys sitting up in the belfry, and went around back and climbed up beside them. Just then the bells started ringing and ringing. A whole procession of Indians dressed as animals and Spaniards emerged from the church door below us. The bells brought everyone running and the procession actually got squeezed back inside again. Some of the donkey heads and conquistador helmets were knocked off in the scuffle. Finally the bells stopped ringing and the Indians went back to their buying and selling and drinking *chicha* beer.

I had a panoramic view of the entire Indian encampment, of the hobbled horses and llamas and herds of sheep grazing beyond, of the wide sweep of the red plain up to the gray hills and icy mountains. I felt I was looking down upon the whole social order of the Indians. They understand society as the source of personality, in which everyone has a place and expression. It unites them with the universe. It is within and for their society that they live and create. No one is left out. Watching from my position in the belfry, I envied them.

The boys climbed down and I stretched out beneath the bell and fell asleep. Someone down below must have pulled the rope by mistake, for the bell jangled briefly with a tinny sound and woke me up. The sun had lowered and now the façade cast a long shadow, in which I could see my own form seated in the aperture beneath the bell. There seemed to be less noise and activity on the plain. Maximilian was leaning against the truck so I climbed slowly down. I'm always reluctant to leave a place which affords a good view of the surrounding area.

As the truck loaded up with our passengers I ate a dish of sheep's liver, onions and rice, and some of those small purple potatoes. Several miles beyond lay the village where the real celebrations were to take place, the scene on the plain being only a prelude to this. The low adobe houses, the numbers of horses, and the fact that everyone wears a wide hat gives this Sierra village the appearance of a wild west town. Big general stores sell Indian blankets, shawls, felt hats, and shotguns. The

Indians were streaming in now by the hundreds, the women with their long braids and long skirts, the men in ponchos and knee breeches. They pass silently through the streets.

As soon as the sun went down it began to get bitter cold. Around the main square steaming cauldrons of tripe stew had been set up. I had brought along a bottle of pisco and began to drink it down. After all, the wind was beginning to blow and everyone else in this town was completely drunk. Some Indians lay face down in the dust. Nobody was smiling. Around a corner sheltered from the wind a man played mountain music on a flute and drum. I was the only one who paid him any attention. He played on and on, stamping his bare foot on the hardened earth. Music is the most articulate sound I ever heard come out of these Indians.

By this time I had drunk down most of the pisco and felt I could sleep anywhere. I followed Maximilian and Pepina down a side street, through a trapezoidal door, and into a windowless room where at least one hundred Indians were sleeping on the floor. The air was so close that I was sure that all the oxygen had been breathed up long ago. Maximilian and Pepina threw their ponchos down.

"Maximilian, are you going to sleep here?"

"There's no other place, Caffery."

"But there's no air in here. You may suffocate during the night."

"Either here or in the street."

We crept among the Indians. At least it was warm in here, and if I kept my head near the open door I wouldn't suffocate. Wedged in among the bodies I lay awake for a long time listening to the sounds a hundred Indians can make while sleeping in the same room. Not many hours remained until dawn. All I wanted was enough daylight to get out of these mountains and back to Lima. Towards morning firecrackers began to go off all over town. It sounded as if the revolution had begun.

I was anxious to begin the return trip immediately, but nobody would leave until he had witnessed the main spectacle of this fiesta. The feet of a condor are tied to the back of a bull and the bull is turned loose in the village plaza. I sat up on top the truck and watched, feeling slightly uneasy. The bull charged among the Indians as the condor beat its wings wildly to keep its balance. I kept waiting for the condor to begin taking bites out of the bull, but it didn't. Both animals were terrified of the crowd of drunken Indians that chased them around.

■ ■ ■

I was glad to be back at the hacienda and to resume work on the dam. In another month the last stones were cemented along the rim, Maximilian's path built against the north cliff, and I was able to close the culvert. As the level of the water rose, Indians appeared to observe the formation of this new body of water. A few minor leaks developed near the base, but as I was wondering what to do about them they sealed themselves off. When the water began to fall away over the dam a murmur of approval went up from the assembled Indians squatting on their heels along the path. I paced back and forth along the top of the dam and finally just jumped in for a swim. The water was clear and cool and deep. All that heavy work in the dust and sun now seemed worth while.

Sr. Alvarado arrived from Lima a few days later, and I took him to have a look at the dam. We remained up there the whole day. He wanted to stock the lake with trout and have a boat to row. Trees and bushes ought to be planted along Maximilian's path to hold the soil. The twenty-foot waterfall excited him, like everyone else, and he estimated that there was enough power to produce electricity for the farm. A small turbine might be set up, which could turn a generator.

In the late afternoon we rode back down the valley. Sr. Alvarado announced that he'd seen Bonsal in Lima and had invited him to the farm. He would arrive tomorrow. Although I hadn't seen him in some time, I had thought about Paul often. I looked forward to showing him the dam.

The next afternoon I drove down to the highway and parked the truck off the road. A man was clearing drifted sand away. Several hundred yards to the north another worker rested on his shovel. A double line of telephone poles paralleled the road and disappeared with it into the heat and silence. I left the truck, walked out onto the pavement, and looked up and down. Seeing the road thus, empty and laked over with shimmering mirages, reminded me of when I used to travel with Anne. A wind was coming in off the sea and whistled among the telephone wires. The shovel scraped and the old man cast the sand into the air, allowing the wind to carry it away. Up the road the other had his legs cut off by the low blowing sand. The old Indian came up to ask me for a cigarette. He had a smooth face and a hard hand.

I'd come too early and waited impatiently for an hour. At last the bus arrived and Bonsal got out. He was wearing the brown leather coat he'd bought in Argentina. I stepped forward, took the suitcase, and carried it to the truck.

"Is this your truck, Caffery?"

"No. I sold mine to Halito with the farm."

"I thought it looked different."

The bus rolled away to the north. The old man stood on the edge of the highway, leaning on his shovel and smoking.

"I hear you've become an engineer and are building a dam."

"That's right. It's finished now and the lake behind it has filled up. You can see right down to the bottom."

"I'm looking forward to seeing it."

"I've been waiting to show it to you. I think it's going to last a long time, unless one of those flash floods knocks it down."

"Flash floods?"

"According to Señor Alvarado it rains plenty up in the Andes and something called *huaicos* are common. Mudslides. They block the river until it breaks through in a torrent. The dam is supposed to arrest them. It sounds pretty dangerous."

"I didn't know they had floods around here."

"That's what I thought, too."

We climbed into the truck but I didn't start the motor immediately. Paul handed me a cigarette.

"Caffery, I've heard that girl Anne has her own cattle farm in Tarapoto now. Anita Juarez has given her some land to work and she's making it into something."

"Perhaps she has the right answer. There's so much good land in this country, you might as well buy some and live on it."

I started up the motor and we drove back to the farm. As Sr. Alvarado was still out in the fields, Paul said he would take a short siesta. I went out to feed the peacocks. They were sitting in the lower branches of the pine trees and didn't seem interested in food. Anyway, it's impossible to sling grain at birds ten feet over your head. I scattered it on the ground and went away. To waste more time I walked out across the dusty soccer field, kicking stones about. A peculiar stillness prevailed over the valley. Normally a wind begins to blow at this hour. I waited. At last came the sound of horses. In the settling darkness Sr. Alvarado and Maximilian came riding past where I sat.

Before dinner Sr. Alvarado mixed up several rounds of pisco sours. As it was an especially warm night we sat out a long time on the veranda. Later two nuns, one old and the other quite young, joined us for dinner. They had come to the hacienda for a few days to give injections to the Indians. The younger one had not yet taken her final vows, and, judging from the way she carried on at the table, I doubted she ever would. She seemed fascinated with Maximilian's beard and the way he had to hold on to it to keep it out of his food. I later heard that she never did take her vows. As usual everything came to the table fresh from the farm. After dinner the nuns disappeared, and we drank whiskey until Maximilian got to his feet and announced that it was time for him to return to his house and to Pepina. As talk that evening had largely concerned the new dam, Paul declared he was ready to have a look at it right now. It was already past midnight, but this seemed like a good idea.

The four of us got into the truck and drove as far as the river. Under the headlights we managed to cross one at a time in Sr. Alvarado's cable car. Maximilian came last in the dark. From there we continued on foot. A late moon had risen behind the mountain. The cacti and boulders cast dim shadows across our path. The air was still warm and heavy, unusual for a desert night. After a while we began to straggle out. Bonsal and Sr. Alvarado walked far ahead; I overheard them speaking Spanish together.

We passed into the ravine and the dam loomed up ahead. Bonsal remarked that he hadn't realized that it was so big, and I had to admit it looked impressive in the darkness. One after another we climbed up Maximilian's path and looked out over the lake. Taking a long drink at the pisco bottle he had brought along, Bonsal declared he was ready for a swim right now, and began taking off his clothes. The lake appeared black and dangerous to me, but perhaps the cold water would clear my head. Soon we had all plunged in and were swimming wildly about. The water felt much warmer than I had anticipated and we stayed in a long time. Finally I dragged myself out and lay down on the dam while the others were getting dressed. Although they were calling to me I dozed off, dreaming that Sr. Alvarado's peacocks were sitting in the branches of the pine tree and making their terrible screeching noise. Suddenly Maximilian caught hold of my arm and dragged me off the dam.

The four of us stood with our backs flat to the rock as a curious rain of small rocks tumbled over the cliff and splashed down into the lake. A strange stillness followed, in which nobody spoke a word or moved. I was shivering all over and not only because I was naked in the night air. All my senses were at work. The initial shock passed and I heard Maximilian shouting that we had better get out from under this cliff, as another tremor might bring it down on us. The others ran off while I gathered up my clothes. I hadn't taken more than a few steps when a shattering roar caused me to drop the clothes. Stupid with fear and confusion, I bent down to pick them up again, wondering whether I should go back and save the dam, wondering where a safe place was. Maximilian was shouting once more in the distance. By the time I caught up with Sr. Alvarado, who had waited for me, I was breathing hard and my bare feet were sore from all the sharp rocks.

We were both so scared that speech was almost impossible, but Sr. Alvarado got it out that the roar of the landslide had come from Maximilian's valley, and he and Paul had rushed off in that direction. I put on my clothes and we ran after them.

I never ran so far or so hard in all my life. Once I stumbled and fell as Sr. Alvarado pounded by. Neither of us spoke; our hard breathing was the only sound in that valley. The cacti and century plants with black stalks sticking up into the night sky stood silently as we ran by. I was so dislocated that for a moment I thought we had come up the wrong valley. However, the high rock bluff behind Maximilian's house became visible. I was looking for the whitewashed square in the darkness, for the pale light of the lantern through the open window, but could make out neither. I was wondering what to do next when I heard Maximilian shouting.

"Pepina! Pepina!" His voice rolled down the valley.

A minute later we saw a white shirt moving in the darkness. A musty smell of dust hung in the air. Then I almost ran into Bonsal, who appeared from behind a boulder.

"What's happened? Where's the house?"

"The landslide destroyed it."

"Where's Pepina?"

"She was inside."

"Pepina!"

Our voices sounded calm and resonant compared to Maximilian's repeated cries.

"Pepina!"

We were standing beside a great pile of rubble that had slid down from the mountainside. In the moonlight I could discern pieces of whitewashed adobe among the rocks.

We searched among the boulders, lighting matches and bringing the others clambering over stones and wreckage when we thought we had found something. Sometimes we called back and forth, sometimes we whispered among ourselves. But it was futile. The moon went down and it became impossible to see anything. And all this time Maximilian kept up his ceaseless calling, as if he saw Pepina's face everywhere. To listen to him carry on like that, his lone cries echoing out into the night, answerless, made one feel slightly mad, like himself.

"Pepina!"

I wanted to tell him to stop this wild shouting for her, as if she couldn't have heard him the first time.

Towards dawn we gave up and waited for the new light to aid our search. Nobody spoke. The silence was broken only by Maximilian's snuffling. I fell asleep.

I was awakened by the sun shining in my eyes. Everyone was still in the same uncomfortable positions, slumped against boulders or sprawled out on the ground. We were all covered with dust and looked as if we had just completed some terrible trek across the desert. But Maximilian looked the worst. He lay on his back with his arms stretched out, snoring loudly through the open mouth. His beard was all matted, and beneath each eye the dry dust had been streaked with tears.

I got stiffly to my feet and looked around. The sun revealed clearly what had happened. Behind where the house used to be the entire bluff had a new face of fresh unweathered rock. A whole vertical slab of rock had fallen away during the tremor and, driving down the slope below, had carried the house before it like driftwood on a breaking wave. Thus all the remains of the house were heaped in a broken pile where the slide had terminated, with a few pieces scattered about in the wake. Some of the enormous boulders had plowed furrows in the ground deep enough for a man to hide in.

The others woke up one by one. Paul looked dejectedly at the ruins. "Perhaps she wasn't in there at all."

Maximilian turned to stare at him. "Where else would she be in the middle of the night?"

"Does anybody else live around here?"

"Nobody lives here but ourselves."

We started searching again for the body. Maximilian uncovered a shovel and dug with that. Suddenly he shouted he had found something soft under the rocks and soil. We ran over.

"What is it?"

He dug further.

"The dog."

Soon the day began to be hot and our sweat mixed with the light dust. Without my straw hat I felt a little dizzy and sat down to rest. Perhaps I hadn't yet regained all my strength.

When I felt better I got to my feet and, unnoticed by the others picking over the ruins, walked away across the slope of the hill towards the spring. I wanted a drink of water and besides, Pepina could have been out picking figs after midnight and, hearing the thunder of falling rock, might still be hiding in terror among the fig trees. However, she was nowhere in sight. Taking a drink of spring water that seeped out of the red shale and stealing a fig from Maximilian's tree, I went back. Upon rounding the hill I saw immediately that they had found her. All three men were standing around in a half circle and looking down, as if into an open grave.

Maximilian got down on his hands and knees and began to carefully remove the stones and dust. She was still in her bed. No doubt the roar of the slide had hardly opened her eyes in terror before it was upon her, carrying her and the bed among the crashing walls of the house like a sled downhill. At first it appeared that she had simply smothered in the dust that now blanketed her, for her mouth was full of it. But as Maximilian excavated further, her body was found to be heavily bruised. Yet the only real mark on her was a sharp piece of stone broken off deep into her abdomen. She lay there on her back, looking up with dusty frightened eyes that would not close. The clothes had been torn off her and the form was slim like a boy's, with small breasts spread flat against her chest. The body seemed so fragile, reclining there among the rocks and debris, but so lifeless that it was difficult to imagine that it had ever been alive.

There was nothing to do but disinter her from one grave and put her into another. Maximilian lifted her up like a child and bore the rather stiff form to the spring, saying it was a place where she liked to pass the time when he was away. Besides, the ground was much softer there. While he sat beside her in the shade of the wild fig tree, absent-mindedly arranging her braided hair and what remained of her clothes, we three took turns working in the sun. I never realized it required such a long time to dig a grave, how long and wide and deep a hole has to be before you can put a body into it. We were at it nearly the whole morning. Finally we lowered her down as gently as possible. Maximilian took one last look at her slightly crumpled body at the bottom of the damp hole, and without another word we commenced to cover her up.

Single file we trailed slowly back down the valley, each one bearing some possession of Maximilian found intact among the wreckage. I had the shovel over my shoulder. Sr. Alvarado led, followed by Paul and myself, with Maximilian lagging in the rear. It was the hottest hour of the day. The sun glared down on the gray cacti and red rocks too hot to touch. The landscape wavered until I was dizzy looking at it. Several times I waited for Maximilian to catch up while the others walked on. His long legs moved heavily, his boots scuffing the light dust.

"Maximilian, what will you do now?"

His mouth opened and closed. There was dust on his lips, foam at the corners of the mouth. "I don't know."

"I suppose you'll leave."

"Leave what?"

"The hacienda."

"No. I told you I'd done with moving. I'll remain here."

"Where? In this valley?"

He stopped to look around at the ledges and boulder-strewn slopes, his blue eyes squinting against the glare. "No. This valley no longer interests me."

"Oh."

We walked side by side without looking at each other.

"She'd been picking figs."

"In the middle of the night?"

"No, yesterday. They were scattered about among the ruins. Fresh ones."

"I didn't notice."

Maximilian was carrying a small cardboard suitcase, which he shifted from hand to hand. Suddenly the suitcase broke open, spilling old clothes out onto the ground. Among them I noticed some of Pepina's bright-coloured Indian dresses. He got to his knees and scooped them up again, the ends of his long black coat dragging in the dust.

"That landslide didn't leave much unbroken or unburied."

"This was all I could find—these old clothes."

He secured , the suitcase with a piece of string from his pocket.

"What are you going to do with this shovel?"

"It belonged to Pepina. We had some potatoes up there, too."

When we reached the dam I stayed behind to open the culvert. A few leaks had been started and it was necessary to lower the level of the lake to repair them. They were not serious, however, and I was pleased that the dam had survived so well a tremor that had done so much damage. Bonsal remained with me. As the water receded I lay on top of the dam. Bonsal swam, dressed, and smoked his last cigarette. All was quiet.

"Paul, it's lucky you came when you did."

"Why?"

"If we hadn't been celebrating your arrival last night, Maximilian would have been in that bed with Pepina."

"We were celebrating your dam. That's what I came to see."

"Maximilian shouldn't have built his house under that bluff."

"Where should he have built it?"

"On the valley floor."

"Probably he wanted a view."

"But the valley is safer."

"He wasn't thinking about landslides."

"No, I suppose not. I guess he chose the best site."

I looked into the water. It appeared that this lake already had some fish in it.

"Paul, do you think flash floods have the power to break down this dam?"

"The tremor didn't seem to shake it much."

"That's true."

"No flash flood is going to crack it."

"I hope not."

"Don't worry."

"I wonder how that natural bridge fared."

"What natural bridge?"

"There's one a few miles upstream. Some of the workers took me to it one day. They told me it was no Inca bridge."

"Inca bridge?"

"For some reason they wanted to point this out to me. I don't know why."

To repair the dam took longer than I expected. The more closely I examined it the more cracks I found. In the end I emptied out the whole lake to do the job properly. One day Maximilian came riding by, dressed as usual in his long black coat and wide hat. The shovel was strapped to the saddle behind him. He dismounted and sat under the tree which had been moved to the edge of the lake. It was as if nothing had happened.

"Where are you going, Maximilian?"

He wet the cigarette paper with his tongue. "Up the valley. I'm going to try to uncover more of my clothes and whatever else I can find."

"I was wondering what that shovel was for."

"After the landslide I just picked up anything I could find."

"It wasn't much."

"I had no desire to carry more away with me. But now I find that I must have clothes—more than what I'm wearing."

"I'm just about finished here. I'll come with you and help you look."

"No, I'll go alone. I think I'll put something on Pepina's grave, a rock or a piece of wood, so it won't go completely unmarked."

He finished the cigarette and got to his feet.

"Maximilian, with the dam repaired I'll be leaving soon, perhaps tomorrow."

He nodded and looked at his horse. "Where are you headed?"

"Just Lima."

"You'll be coming back here from time to time."

"I'm sure I will."

"I'll be here. I told you I'm not going anywhere."

He got on his horse and rode away without looking back. When he was out of sight I closed the culvert, picked up the tools, and walked back to the hacienda.

The following morning Sr. Alvarado drove Bonsal and me down to the coastal highway. He intended to wait with us, but after an hour we persuaded him to return to the farm. The bus service seems unreliable, especially when you have to wait out in the desert for a bus coming down the coast from a town three or four hundred miles to the north. Bonsal was out on the highway impatiently looking both ways. Sitting down on my suitcase, I told him to relax. I don't mind waiting. The sun was hot and we had no cover, but enough breeze was coming in off the sea to make it comfortable. I felt good, and could have travelled in either direction on that highway. Both looked exactly the same to me, the black tar moving free in the heat patterns until the road seemed to lift right off the ground. Towards noon the heat became oppressive and I was wondering if I ought to take a chance and run down for a swim, when the bus came along.

There were no two seats together, so Bonsal took the one up front next to the driver and I sat in back. Every time I'm out on this road I make a point to keep my eye open for that long straightaway where the pig accident occurred. About two o'clock we passed it. Although there were no pig carcasses turning back into the sand or the wrecked chassis of an old truck, I knew this was the place. On all that long strip of road flanking the sea there was no other place like it. I looked back through the rear window until the road bent off behind a low hill, forcing the straightaway from my sight.

Later on we came to that same town Anne and I had stopped in. The bus pulled up in front of the same restaurant. It was cool inside, as before, and I recognized the man behind the bar. Bonsal knew the place, too. It seemed to me he knew every bar and restaurant in Peru. Anyway, this familiarity put us at ease, and we ate big plates of *seviche* and drank beer. Afterwards I accompanied Bonsal to the market, where he proceeded to bargain with a man over a crate of pears. When they reached a price Bonsal put down his money, hoisted the crate onto his shoulder, and set off back to the bus. I ran along behind him.

"Paul, what are you going to do with all those pears? You can't squeeze them like oranges."

"Never mind. I like pears, never get enough of them."

He staggered under the heavy load, mumbling something about the best pears in Peru.

The bus was still empty, so after taking out a few handfuls we put the pears on top and went back into the bar. The driver was sitting in the corner about to begin his meal. Bonsal shouted something in Spanish and threw a pear at him. The man caught it in one hand, laughed, and put it into his mouth. For the next hour we drank pisco and ate pears, which is a good combination. The driver joined us at the bar. He and Bonsal carried on in Spanish while I gazed at myself in the rusty mirror behind the bar, dully wondering when we would be on the road again.

"Caffery, this man says he knows you."

The bus driver was grinning.

"He says once he left you and a girl off where we got on today—at the intersection with Alvarado's road."

"That was some time ago."

The driver's face now seemed vaguely familiar.

"Tell him he left us off at the wrong place. We were looking for the Valle de las Culebras, which is farther up the highway.

Bonsal translated. I felt too lazy to speak Spanish.

"Isn't that how you met Alvarado? You walked into his hacienda by mistake."

"That's right. Tell him it's just as well he left us off where he did. Otherwise I never would have met Señor Alvarado."

Bonsal translated again. The grin widened.

"Tell him I'm very happy he left us off there."

Back on the bus I stuffed my poncho between the window and my head as a pillow and listened to Bonsal sing a song in Quechua, with the Indians turning round to stare at him. I dozed for a while and when I awoke everyone was asleep. The bus rumbled on as the sun dropped down towards the Pacific. I caught the driver's eyes in the mirror. Now I remembered him.

When I get back to Lima I'm going to find myself a place to live. Something more permanent than the shacks and barges I've been used to. I'm tired of switching around. Over in the old part of town behind the Plaza de Armas there must be some cheap place. I'll get Bonsal to drive me up to one of those country festivals some Sunday or holy day when the Indians get together and buy some Indian blankets. Also I'll need a cactus over the door for good luck. I have some money to live on for a while. Sr. Alvarado gave me plenty for building that dam. Anyway, the point is to keep on living the best I can. Place is important and Peru is as good a place as any.

Mile after mile I scanned the desert for those old billboards, but we must have passed them while I was asleep. We were getting in towards Lima now, the sun was resting on the sea. The odour of fish meal from Callao became faintly noticeable. I don't mind; it's always good to come back into Lima, especially after a long ride down the desert highway. We passed through the Plaza Dos de Mayo, all rutted with trolley tracks. The city was all around us.

The bus unloaded at Parque Universitario. Bonsal, still half asleep and from what I could see still drunk, took the crate of pears on his shoulder and staggered off down the street. I ran after him with the suitcases and ponchos. It was dark now.

"Let's take a taxi, Paul. You'll never be able to carry that crate as far as the apartment."

"Bring the suitcases."

We rambled along the crowded streets past rows of shoeshine stands where young boys and old men in baseball caps snapped their rags or lounged idly in the stalls, reading newspapers. At *colectivo* ranks hoarse drivers shouted destinations, trams rolled by, and old women sat on the pavement, endlessly rearranging piles of avocados. Under his heavy load Bonsal reeled down the sidewalk and the people got out of his way. Following closely, slipping on the avocado peels, I couldn't decide whether he was just staggering drunkenly or purposely dancing to the mountain music blaring loudly from radios.

Our path detoured around Plaza San Martín and led through a park full of palm trees and statues of Peruvian generals lit up by old-time street lamps. We came out at the prison. Here Bonsal put down the crate and leaned up against the red brick wall.

"You've carried it far enough, Paul. Let me carry it for a while."

He shook his head and hoisted it up on his shoulder once more just as I was lighting up a cigarette.

When we entered the apartment he let the crate slam down on the floor. Some pears bounced out and rolled away under the couch. While he was groping for them I stepped out on the terrace. Down the avenue the Coca-Cola sign was going through its routine. The enormous cement Christ shone from a mountain behind the city. The lights of Callao and of ships waiting to enter the harbour glowed dimly from the coast. I was reminded of my return from the jungle, when for the first time I looked out into the summer night from this terrace.

Bonsal stood in the doorway taking a long swig from the pisco jug.

"Come out here and look at this view," I said.

He stepped forward and put the jug down on the wall among the clay pots and bulls and churches he had collected from the Sierra.

"Don't lean on this wall, Caffery. There's a crack in it."

The glass jug caught the red glare from the sign.

"Tell me what you plan to do."

"I think I'll go back to the Pensión Americana."

"Why? It's fine to have your shoes polished there but not much else."

"I miss it in a way."

I lifted up the jug and took a few swallows. The red light was refracted through the glass and into my eyes.

"That's good pisco."

"Why do you miss a place like that?"

"I admit it's not very comfortable but I just got used to it. I plan to look around for a flat. Over near the bull ring would be a good site."

"The river smells."

"The whole city smells."

"The streets are noisy."

"Nothing could be worse than living above the YMCA."

When I set the jug down again Bonsal put out a hand to steady it. The sign blinked and his bare arm turned red.

"If I find a flat, perhaps one day we can take a ride back into the hills to an Indian market. I'd like to pick up a few things."

"You won't find more than blankets and ponchos."

"That's all I want. I used to own a brass bed, sold it to a junk yard, but I think I can get it back. I'll use this flat as a base and start looking again."

"For what?"

"I wouldn't mind starting up a lumbering operation in the jungle or getting involved in something on the coast. I've run cows and built a dam. There ought to be something else I can do. But I'm in no hurry; there are plenty of possibilities."

"I think to be alone in this country is a glorious thing."

"Sometimes I think so."

We agreed to meet at the Swiss restaurant for dinner. Leaving the building I crossed the street and looked up. Bonsal was still there leaning on the wall as he had told me not to do, the glint of the pisco bottle before him. Instinctively I waved to signal that I saw him. He slowly raised his hand in reply, as if he wasn't sure who I was. Then I took a path through the park, past a bandstand and a holy place where some people had gathered, placing branches of pink flowers and lighting candles. I stopped for a moment to watch them, then hurried on past the prison walls. Inexplicably I felt an urgency to be back in the heart of the city.

The shoeshine boys had their backs turned when I entered the courtyard but Rodrigo spotted me coming up the stairs. I got my old room back. When Rodrigo shut the door behind him I lay down on the bed and put my hands behind my head and fell asleep. An hour later I awoke, washed my face in the basin, and went downstairs. For the next half hour I read the newspaper and had my shoes polished. A man paused to light a cigarette in the big Spanish doorway to the street, and for an instant I thought it was Harry. But he turned and showed another face.

I stepped out onto Carabaya and walked down to Plaza San Martín. The lines had already formed in front of the movie houses. There had been a collision by the Hotel Bolivar. People argued and shouted in the street. Meanwhile, amid so much chaos of noise and light, Indians lay stretched out on the grass, using jackets and newspapers for pillows, or sat together talking in a confidential manner. Above these silent forms the neon dice kept rolling down. I crossed the street and was walking along Colmena. Just then the tram, crowded with sailors hanging on, started up. It passed me and headed down to Callao.